GREAT-GRAN'S DIARY

Great-Gran's
Diary

Joan Peake

PONT BOOKS

First Impression—2000

ISBN 1 85902 884 5

© Joan Peake

Printed in Wales at
Gomer Press, Llandysul, Ceredigion SA44 4QL

*In memory of
my mother, Rose*

*And with grateful thanks to Tia, Asmat, Sarah,
Kirsty, Emma, Bethan, Helyn, Kristina
and Lianne—formerly of Gladstone School
and also to the children of Years 5 and 6
of St. Monica's School, Cardiff.*

Chapter 1

Hannah traced the golden inlaid design on the top of the box with loving fingers. It had once been Great-Gran's and for as long as she could remember Hannah had admired it. Its smooth wood felt like silk to her touch.

'You must take great care of it,' Nan said. 'It's very old—an antique, really, so it's quite valuable.'

'Oh, I will,' promised Hannah. 'It's the most beautiful thing I ever had.' She looked at her grandmother searchingly. 'You sure you don't want to keep it yourself? After all, Great-Gran was your mother.'

For a moment Nan's blue eyes were anxious, as if she were afraid Hannah was going to return her gift.

'No, I'd like you to have it. I don't have a daughter to hand it on to. And you like sewing, don't you?'

Hannah nodded in agreement. 'I'm not very good at it, though.'

'That'll come with practice,' Nan said. 'Now, you'd better have a bag to carry it home in. I wouldn't want it to slip out of your hands, or it might split open at the joints.'

'Thanks—and I will be careful,' promised Hannah.

Hannah showed the sewing box to her mother as soon as she got home.

Her mother, looking wistful said, 'Yes, I remember it always had place of honour on Great-Gran's sideboard. She must have used plenty of elbow grease to keep it like that. If I were you, I'd take it upstairs to your bedroom so your brother can't get his hands on it, or it won't last long.'

'He'd better not touch it,' Hannah said, 'or he'll be sorry.'

Once in her bedroom, she sat on the bed and opened the lid. Inside was a shallow tray just deep enough to hold the multi-coloured reels of cotton that Great-Gran had used. Underneath the tray in a tangle lay skeins of embroidery silks, lengths of elastic, a few zips that had been cut out of discarded clothes, a tape measure, safety pins, another small box of pins, a pack containing sewing needles and two pairs of scissors. The blue silk lining of the lid was criss-crossed with braid in the same shade for holding small things in place. Hannah sorted small items that would fit into the loops and immediately the box looked much neater.

Now I can find things easily, she thought. I must ask Mum if she's got any bits of material I can use now I've got a proper sewing kit.

She began to wind the lengths of elastic around her fingers and took out the different coloured silks, laying them side by side on the bed cover.

The bottom of the box had a good deal of debris —fluff, pins, minute pieces of paper and suchlike that had collected there over the ages. Hannah turned the box upside down and, forgetting Nan's instructions to treat it gently, gave it a sharp tap on the corner of the table to eject the rubbish.

She was horrified when it seemed that the bottom of the box had fallen out and instantly regretted her carelessness. Looking again, though, she saw that the wooden bottom was intact, but the piece that had fallen out appeared to be a velvet, padded bottom in a deep plum colour.

How strange, she thought, when the rest of the box is lined in blue. But picking it up, she found that what she held in her hand was a thin, velvet-covered book with a silken ribbon attached which acted as a place mark. The book felt warm to the touch, as if it were a living, breathing thing.

Opening it at the first yellowed page, Hannah read:

'This book was presented to Rose Turner on her tenth birthday by her loving aunt, Lizzie. 20th September, 1914.

Be good sweet maid and let who will be clever,
Do noble deeds not dream them all day long.'

'Wow, I wonder if Nan knew about this,' she said. 'It looks as if it's been there years and years.'

She began to read,

'When Auntie Lizzie gave me this book for my birthday I made a promise to myself that I would write in it every day, but I'll have to keep it safe from Emma and Sidney or they will scribble in it.'

A sentence further down grabbed Hannah's attention:

'So many men want to enlist to fight the Germans that Maindy Barracks couldn't hold them all, so they used Gladstone School as a recruiting station.'

Gladstone School—Hannah's own school!

For a moment Hannah sat and stared at the careful, copperplate script, so different from her own scrawl, then closing the book with a snap rushed down the stairs calling, 'Mum, Mum, look what I've found!'

Her mother was sitting at her computer in the corner of the living room she used as her office. Files and books lined the shelves in the alcove above her and on the side of the desk was a stand holding sheets of hand-written paper from which she was copying, her fingers flying over the keys.

She swivelled round on her chair,

'What's all the noise about?' she asked. 'Is the house on fire?'

Hannah laughed. 'No, but look what I've found in the bottom of the box Nan gave me.'

She held out the book, but her mother was frowning at the screen again. 'Hold on a minute, I've nearly finished this thesis for that student, but this bit's tricky.'

Hannah waited, jigging from one foot to the other until her mother turned round again to face her.

'Now, what is it?'

'It's a book. I found it in the bottom of the sewing box. It's a diary. It was Great-Gran's when she was the same age as me—and guess what?'

'I don't know. What?'

'It looks as if she went to Gladstone, too. See! It says here, about using the school as a recruiting centre for the army.'

'Let me see!'

She took the book from Hannah and began to read.

'Yes,' she said slowly. 'I knew she went to Gladstone—in fact, you're the fourth generation to go there. I didn't know there was a diary at the bottom of that box, though. The times I've looked in there for a needle to sew on a button or to get a safety pin when we've been in Nan's house! I wonder if she knew it was there?'

'I'll go and tell her, shall I?' Hannah asked,

almost out of the door before her mother could answer.

'No, not now. It's your turn to lay the table—and I know you, if you go to Nan's, you'll be there for hours. Wait 'til later.'

'But she'd want to see it. It belonged to her mother.'

'If it's been there that long it can wait a bit longer. Now, wash your hands and lay the table, while I save this. The timer's just gone off on the oven, so the pie's ready for tea. And you'd better put this book somewhere safe. You wouldn't buy anything like this nowadays, not with a padded velvet cover. Very elegant!'

When Hannah's father came home, she told him about her find as soon as he came through the front door.

'Oh, sounds interesting. Let's have a look.'

Hannah took the book out of the tapestry canvas bag in which she carried her things to school.

'Here it is. Look, it says she was ten when she started to write it, same age as me! I was going to take it straight round to Nan's, but I think I'll read it first. I don't s'pose Great-Gran would mind, would she?'

'We-ell, it was written ages ago and any secrets in it are long forgotten—and if this thing about using the school as a recruiting centre is anything to go by, it could be interesting.'

'Yes, that's what I thought, bit like a history lesson only better. Did you see this about tipping the washing out on the grass when she and her sister were taking it home to be washed? I bet she got a row!'

'Mmm, things don't change much, do they?'

'I hope Nan'll let me keep it. I wonder if she knew it was there, but has forgotten about it?'

'We'll pop round there later and ask her while Tim's getting ready for bed. But first let's have tea; I'm starving. Where's Tim? Better call him in from the garden. It'll take half an hour to get the mud off him!'

DIARY

This book was presented to
Rose Turner
on her tenth birthday
by her loving aunt, Lizzie.
20th September, 1914

'Be good sweet maid and let who will be clever,
Do noble deeds not dream them all day long.'

September 20th, 1914.

When Auntie Lizzie gave me this book for my birthday, I made a promise to myself that I would write in it every day. I'll have to keep it safe from Emma and Sidney or they will scribble in it.

Mama is very worried: someone saw Len hanging around the barracks again. He's been saying he wants to join the army ever since war broke out. He can't really because he's only fourteen, but Mama is afraid he will try to put his age on to enlist.

There are so many men wanting to join up that Maindy Barracks couldn't hold them all, so they used my school, Gladstone, as a recruiting station. They didn't give us a holiday, though.

Sept. 21st.

Me and Lillian took a basket of clean washing up to Colchester Avenue today and on the way back we tipped the dirty sheets we'd brought back with us to wash out on to the grass in the Recreation Ground and dragged each other round in the basket. The two Miss Rawlingses, whose sheets they were, saw us and said they were going to tell Mama. They said we ought to be ashamed of ourselves when Mama has to work so hard. Anyone could tell they are schoolteachers, just by the way they talk. The things had to be washed anyway, so we didn't think it would matter, but when we told Mama what had happened she said she'd have to boil them longer in the copper to get the stains out. Of course, I got the blame. Mama said that I, as the eldest, should be able to be trusted to do a little job for her without getting into mischief.

Chapter 2

'Well, this is a surprise! Two visits in one day.' Nan's hair was tousled and Hannah laughed as she reached up to pull a twig from amongst the faded blonde strands. A muddy streak at the corner of her grandmother's blue eyes traced where she had rubbed one of the canvas gardening gloves she wore.

'Come in, come in,' she said. 'I've been trying to dig out some of the brambles that've come up under the wall. That man next door does nothing to his garden and makes twice as much work for me. What with the dandelion seeds floating over and taking root and other things tunnelling under the wall, I've got to be at it all the time! Just let me wash my hands and I'll be with you. Go in and sit down. I'll put the kettle on.'

Hannah and her Dad went into the cosy living room where the evening sun still streamed through the open window and as she sank down on to the soft cushions of the sofa, Hannah could hear a blackbird singing in the apple tree at the bottom of the garden.

Nan came back a few moments later with clean hands, but with the muddy streak still under her eye.

'Right, that's done. Now then . . .' She waited expectantly.

'We came to tell you that Hannah found something in that workbox you gave her that she thought you ought to see—or perhaps you knew it was there and had forgotten about it?'

'Oh, what's that?'

'This,' Hannah said, pulling the slim volume out of her pocket.

Nan frowned. 'What is it?' she asked, holding out her hand to take it from her.

'Look,' Hannah rose and opened it at the first page. 'See? This book belongs to Rose Turner—that's your mother, isn't it? It's her diary. Did you know it was there?'

'Where? In the workbox?' asked Nan.

'Yes. I thought it was padding on the bottom, but when I tipped everything out, it turned out to be this!'

Nan reached for her glasses, then leaning back in her chair, began to read.

'Well, well,' she said, at last. 'To think this has been there all that time.'

'Would it be all right if I read it? Dad said he didn't think you'd mind.'

'It's so long ago,' explained her Dad. 'It's not like prying into someone else's diary; it's more like a piece of history. There's even something about her brother wanting to join up in the First World War.'

'Is there really?' said Nan. 'No, I don't see anything wrong in reading it. But would you mind if I read it first? It won't take me long. You can have it back tomorrow.'

'Oh, good. Wait 'til I tell Laura I've got an antique sewing box and that I found an antique diary in it!'

Nan and her father laughed and Hannah thought how alike they were. Their faces were the same shape with bright blue eyes and slightly tip-tilted noses and they laughed at the same things.

Nan said, 'Let's have a drink, shall we? I'm parched after all that digging. What'll it be? Tea or coffee? And what about you, Hannah. Lemonade and a biscuit?'

Next day, Hannah couldn't wait to tell her best friend about her find.

'My Nan gave me a beautiful sewing box. It's got a design in different coloured wood on the top and there's all these silks and things in it.'

'Why did your Nan give it to you? Doesn't she want it herself?'

'She's got one. This one wouldn't be big enough for her; she's always sewing or knitting. 'Sides, she wanted me to have it. It was my Great-Gran's. A family heirloom, sort of.'

'Oh. I see.'

Hannah could tell by Laura's voice that she wasn't very impressed. Laura was more interested in her Disney figures collection than sewing.

'That's not all, though. Guess what I found in the bottom?'

'A pearl necklace?'

Hannah pushed her long brown hair behind her ears impatiently and sighed.

'No-o. Don't be silly. You wouldn't find a pearl necklace in a sewing box, now, would you? Although you wouldn't think what I found there would be there either. If you see what I mean.'

Laura put on her bored face. 'You gonna tell me or what?'

'Well, I've found out that when Great-Gran was a little girl she wrote a diary and hid it in the bottom of the box so her little brother and sister wouldn't find it. She must have forgotten all about it—but I found it last night!'

'Oh, I thought you were going to say it was something exciting.'

'Well, it is! And guess what! She used to come to this school, too!'

'Wow! Big deal—any more wonderful secrets in it?'

Hannah decided to ignore Laura's sarcastic remarks.

'I dunno yet. Nan's reading it at the moment.

Even she didn't know it was there and she's had the box for ages. I discovered it!'

Just then the school bell rang for them to line up in the playground which put an end to their discussion for the time being. But once they were inside, Hannah began talking about her find again, much to Laura's annoyance.

'Oh, I don't know why you're so excited about an old diary. It's not like having a new doll or something. Did I tell you about the one I'm having for my birthday? It's the best one yet—a collector's item my Mum says. It's got a red velvet dress and a hat to match and it's even got a muff to keep its hands warm. I saw it in Mum's catalogue and she's going to get it for me.'

'You girls! What's all the chat about? Settle down now and get your books out.'

'It's Hannah, Miss Edwards. She found some old diary belonging to her Great-Gran and she hasn't stopped talking about it since we came to school.'

'Well, I think I'd be excited if I found something like that. D'you want to tell the class about it, Hannah?'

Pulling a face at Laura, Hannah stood up and told everyone how she had come to find the diary.

'I didn't know 'til I started to read it that my Great-Gran used to come to this school—and her brothers and sisters did. I don't know everything that's in it, 'cause I haven't read it all yet.'

'I can understand why you're excited. Perhaps you would like to bring it to school and we can see if there is anything else about Gladstone in it?'

Hannah nodded enthusiastically. At least her teacher was interested in her find!

Nan had returned the diary while her granddaughter was at school and left a message with Hannah's mother to say that she had read it and to make sure Hannah didn't lose it because she was making a family tree and the diary might be useful in sorting out the relatives.

When she went to bed that night Hannah took out the diary and again felt the warmth of the velvet in her hands. It was as if the book was glad to have escaped its long years in the dust on the bottom of the box.

She opened it on the second page and began to read. Her eyes opened in amazement when she read how different the school had been in Great-Gran's day. They'd a stove like the one she'd seen in cowboy films standing in the middle of the classroom and the caretaker had come in to make up the fire at playtime. And fancy having to bring your own milk to school if you needed it!

She fell asleep thinking of the delicate little girl

who had been Great-Gran's sister and whose mother had given her a medicine bottle of milk for her teacher to put on the stove to warm her.

Next day, she took the diary to school, tucking it carefully into her bag so that it wouldn't fall out.

Mum had said she didn't think Hannah ought to take it. 'It belongs to all the family, really,' she'd said, 'and it would be awful if you lost it. You know how careless you are with things. Remember that ring of mine I let you borrow!'

'I won't lose it, I promise,' Hannah pleaded, 'and, anyway, I told Miss Edwards I'd take it to show her. She said she'd like to see it—it would be interesting.'

Hannah's eyes pricked with tears at the threatened disappointment and the thought of letting Miss Edwards down. She had been so enthusiastic about her diary; how could she face her if her mother wouldn't let her take it?

'Go on, then,' her mother said, 'but take care of it!'

Miss Edwards looked pleased when Hannah showed her Great-Gran's diary. 'What a lovely cover!' she said. 'We'll read a little bit out of it later. In the meantime, get your maths books out and turn to page forty.'

Hannah looked up and saw Miss Edwards studying the diary while the class were doing their maths. She seemed to be reading very intently and it was only when Iwan Davies put his hand up and said he couldn't do one of the sums, that she put the book down reluctantly and went to help him.

Miss Edwards read out some of the entries that mentioned the school during their English lesson and the class listened quietly.

She picked out the bit about Great-Gran being afraid that her Headmistress would punish her for being late and how her sister had been caned for talking in lines.

'I wonder how many of you would have the cane if it was still in use now?' she said with a grin. 'I can think of quite a few!'

That afternoon after lunch, Miss Edwards said, 'I hope you don't mind, Hannah, but I showed your diary to Mr Harris at lunchtime and—you know it's the school's centenary soon, don't you?'

Hannah shook her head.

'Well, if you look outside on the wall of the building, you'll see a date carved on a block of lighter stone there and it says 1900—and of course the school's centenary will be the Millennium year too.'

Hannah remembered the date on the diary's first page. 1914. It was quite a new school when her Great-Gran came here, then—nearly a hundred years ago.

'Anyway,' said Miss Edwards. 'Mr Harris is very keen to celebrate the school's history in some way and after seeing your diary he thought it would be a good idea to have a competition. It will be sort of project where everyone will try to find out as much about the school as they possibly can and there'll be a prize for the person who comes up with the most interesting and well-written one. You'll have a head start with your Great-Gran's diary, won't you?'

That's exactly what Hannah was thinking herself!

Sept. 25th.

Emma doesn't like school. She cried all the way there this morning. Mama gave me a medicine bottle full of milk to give to her teacher to put on the stove so she can have a warm drink at playtime. Mama is very worried about her, she is so thin, not like the rest of us. Her teacher said she would let her sit nearest the stove in the winter when it's lit. Lucky dab! Everybody wants to sit in the front when it's cold, although it smells of rotten eggs when the caretaker stokes it up with coke at playtime.

Sept. 30th.

Late for school this afternoon. Miss Hemmings caught me as I went into the cloakroom. I thought she'd be sure to give me the cane, but she just told me to be more punctual. I think she knows somehow that I have to clean the

grate at dinnertime, ready to light the fire by the time Dada comes home at night. Lillian had the cane for only talking in lines the other day. I didn't think that was fair.

Oct. 7th.

I'm not keeping my diary as I should, but there's not much time after helping Mama with the younger ones. I had ten out of ten, excellent for my sums today and Miss Davies said she was very pleased with my work. Then in the next breath, she scolded me for blotting my copy book. I couldn't help it: the nib on my pen crossed and the ink splattered.

Oct. 15th.

I nearly had all my hair burnt off last night, thanks to Lillian. Mama let me carry the candle to light us up to bed and Lillian pushed past me on the stairs, jolting my arm and setting one of my curling rags on fire. Mama was close behind and put out the flames. Lucky for me, my hair was still damp, but Mama burnt her hands.

Oct. 16th.

I got my own back on Lillian for singeing my hair. The back bedroom door was ajar as we came up tonight and the sleeve of Reggie's coat, which was hanging on the back of the door, blew into the opening as we passed. I grabbed Lillian's arm and pointed. She thought there was a man in the bedroom and screamed for Dada. He wasn't very pleased to be disturbed by 'the silly girl'.

Oct. 19th.

Mama and Dada went to see Auntie Lizzie. Mama left me in charge and made us promise to behave ourselves. We decided to borrow her lace curtains to dress up and play 'brides', but of course, Lillian had to catch her heel in one of them and ripped it. Mama was upset and Dada was very cross. He said they'd never be able to go out again because he couldn't trust us. But he blamed me most of all because I'm the eldest girl. It's not fair.

Oct. 21st.
Only the usual things happened.

Oct. 30th.
Mama said that if we're very good we can have a Bob-Apple party tomorrow night. I do try very hard, but Dada always picks on me. He even blamed me when Mama burnt her hands.

Oct. 31st.
Had a lovely time at our Bob-Apple party. Mama filled the zinc bath she bathes the little ones in with cold

water, then she floated some of the apples she had from Somerset in it and we had to try and catch them with our teeth. No hands allowed; we had to keep them behind our backs. Len kept pushing our heads under the water and the kitchen floor was swimming afterwards. Good job Dada had gone to the pictures! After that, Mama tied some of the apples on a string and hung them from a line across the kitchen. If we managed to bite one we could eat it. We had a mug of cocoa before going to bed and sat round the fire telling ghost stories. Lillian frightened Emma and Margaret so much they were afraid to go upstairs to bed. They made so much noise going up the stairs, they woke Sidney and we were all in trouble.

Chapter 3

With the thought of the project competition in mind, Hannah settled down that evening to study the diary. As she read about Great-Gran singeing her hair, she began to wonder what it must have been like in those days with no electric light on the stairs. In her mind's eye she saw the children climbing upstairs by the light of a flickering candle.

It must have been creepy in the dark corners where the light didn't reach and there would have been weird shadows cast as draughts caught the flame. No wonder Lillian had been frightened when the sleeve of her brother's coat was blown around the door. She had probably thought they were being attacked by a burglar! Great-Gran had certainly paid her sister back for setting her curling rags on fire.

But what a dismal life she must have led! Imagine having to go home at lunchtime to blacklead the grate and clean out the ashes, because that was what Nan said they had to do every day when people had coal fires. She probably got herself very dirty doing it—and Nan said they only had cold water in the taps. All the

31

hot water they needed would have to be boiled in kettles or in the copper on washdays.

There was obviously no heat in the house until evening, because Great-Gran had mentioned that the fire was laid 'by the time Dada comes home at night'. Hannah reached out and felt the warm radiator on her bedroom wall. Poor Great-Gran!

Of course, they'd had some fun, too, dressing up. And the Hallowe'en party when they'd bobbed for apples, sounded wonderful.

As she read, Hannah's interest grew. It was like being a detective: the more she read, the more facts emerged and began to form themselves into a picture. And the more she learned, the more she wanted to know.

She began to feel close to Great-Gran. After all, she had been the same age as her when she wrote her diary, but it was not just because of that, it was almost as if Great-Gran lived again through the pages of the book and became real to her. Hannah began to see her school and the streets and shops through Great-Gran's eyes.

Next morning in class, she took the book out of her bag, feeling the soft texture of the velvet. To think that Great-Gran had once held this book in her hands. She had probably sat in this very classroom! Hannah gently stroked the pile of the material, wondering what Great-Gran had thought about as she sat here doing her lessons. Perhaps she had been worrying when her pen nib crossed and blotted her copy book .

As Hannah smoothed the diary, her surroundings began to change. She had a strange, dream-like picture of the entire school. In the Assembly Hall, the stage, curtains and colourful drawings on the walls—some the work of Hannah's class—began to fade away, to be replaced by paintings depicting stories from the Bible.

In the classroom, she saw rows of desks, instead of tables grouped together where her class sat, and at the front a tall desk stood on a small platform where the teacher worked.

And the teacher! She was a stern-looking lady wearing a dress made of some dark stuff right down to her ankles. Her long hair was plaited and pulled into a coronet around her head.

Hanging over the blackboard was a willowy, cream-coloured cane!

Gone were the nature posters; the model houses they'd made out of clay, then painted; and the pictures they'd copied from postcards of old Masters. Instead, there was one picture of the 'Good Shepherd' which Hannah knew the name of because she had seen one exactly like it in Sunday School. The rest of the walls were painted a dark green to waist level, and were absolutely bare.

The children looked different too. Instead of T-shirts, trousers or skirts and trainers, the girls wore white pinafores, with frills over the shoulders, covering dark dresses, while upstairs in the boys' school they mostly wore knitted jerseys and dark trousers which reached below their knees. All wore buttoned or laced-up boots. They sat bolt upright, their arms folded across their chests as they listened to what their teachers were saying.

The classrooms seemed darker and gloomier than Hannah's, in spite of the fact that the windows and doors were exactly the same size as they were today. And there, in the middle of the room, stood the pot-bellied iron stove, its big, black flue going up through the ceiling, just the way that Great-Gran had written about it. Probably just like the one her little sister's milk had warmed on.

A book falling to the floor with a bang brought Hannah back to the present. She shook her head and blinked her eyes—and everything was back exactly as it usually was. Had it been a dream? She stole a look around her. No one seemed to have noticed anything unusual. She heaved a sigh of relief. It would have been hard to explain if she had been sleeping in class—but had she?

Laura looked up, 'What do you make the answer to number five?' she asked.

'Oh, dunno. I haven't done it yet.'

Laura gave her a funny look.

'You all right? You look as if you've seen a ghost!'

Hannah laughed. 'I can't imagine ghosts living here,' she said. But then thought to herself, *What if they did?* She tried to picture all the children who had come to her school since it opened—there must have been thousands! Their ghosts could be milling around everywhere. What would they make of the computers, the electric light, telephones and calculators? They wouldn't have a clue what they were for.

Hannah was last finishing her maths that morning.

'What's the matter, Hannah? It's not like you; you're usually one of the first to finish. Not finding the work difficult, are you?' Miss Edwards gave her a searching look.

'No, Miss. I was thinking . . .'

'But not about your work, eh? You must concentrate. You weren't late going to bed, were you?'

'No, Miss.' Hannah hadn't been late going to bed, but she had been reading the diary long past the time her light should have been out. Perhaps that was why she had seen the vision—she was tired and had had a sort of waking dream.

She called in to see her Nan on the way home. She'd had an idea.

'Nan, what was Great-Gran's house like? Where did she live?'

'Why d'you want to know that? Is it something to do with the diary?'

'Well, sort of.' Hannah went on to tell Nan about the strange experience she'd had in school that day. 'I could see it all. The stove, the children and the way they dressed, everything!'

'I see . . .' Nan was thoughtful. 'And what has that got to do with where she lived?'

'I wondered if I could go there, see if the same thing happened.'

Nan laughed. 'I doubt it. Anyway, you couldn't very well ask the present owners to let you look over their house, now could you?'

'There might be some way . . .'

'No, Hannah, you're not to bother people. It wouldn't be right. Anyway, you probably dozed off for a couple of seconds in class. If you've been reading that diary late into the night, you were probably tired.'

'Mmm, I thought that too. But it was so real!'

'Well, wait and see. If all you want is to see what kind of house my mother lived in, I may be able to arrange it. But I wouldn't talk about what you thought you saw, if I were you. People may not understand.'

'All right. D'you know someone living in Great-Gran's house then?'

'Not in the same house, but one like it. I'm not promising, mind you, but I'll try.'

Hannah chuckled to herself as she walked home. Nan had said she mustn't worry people, then in the next breath she had said she'd help her. She must want to know more about the diary's 'magic', too.

Then she thought, I'll just have a look through it again tonight to see if there's any clue to where Great-Gran lived, just in case Nan can't wangle that invitation.

Chapter 4

Next day, remembering Great-Gran's reference to 'The Terrace', Hannah decided to walk home that way.

She looked round continually to see if there were any people she knew. There was only one, a girl called Selina who had not been at the school very long and who seemed to have taken a dislike to her. Hannah didn't know what she had done to upset her, but if Selina had a chance to be nasty towards her, she took it.

Hannah looked at the girl's solitary figure and wondered if it would be any use trying to make friends with her. Something inside her gave a nervous little flutter at the thought. Selina had an awful temper, probably because her red hair had drawn all kinds of name-calling from some children, especially the boys, who called her 'Carrots' and 'Ginger', but Hannah had never joined in and couldn't understand why Selina took it out on her.

Almost against her will, she found herself crossing the road and falling into step with the girl. The longing to find out more about Great-Gran was stronger than the fear of a rebuff.

'Hi!' she said, forcing a smile.

Selina turned and frowned.

'D'you live down here then?'

'I wouldn't be going this way if I didn't, would I?'

Hannah chewed on her lip, but went on.

'My Great-Gran used to live off The Terrace somewhere.'

'Yeah? What am I supposed to do about that? Turn cartwheels?'

'It's just that I'm trying to find out where she lived.'

'Well, it's no good asking me. We haven't lived here long.' And without so much as a smile or 'goodbye', Selina turned off down a side street and left Hannah gazing after her.

She wished she hadn't spoken to the girl. Selina must really hate her to treat her like this! Hannah tried to push the unpleasant scene out of her mind and decided to make for home. She would be late as it was and her mother would be anxious. Perhaps another day, when she had more time. But before she came again she would finish reading the diary to see if there were any other clues to Great-Gran's address.

She crossed the road again, turned down a side street and hurried home.

'Wherever have you been?' Her mother's face wore an expression of relief, mixed with annoyance. 'I was passing the school and decided to walk home with you. I waited ages, then someone said you'd gone, yet I got home before you. You didn't come straight home, did you?'

It was a rule that Hannah must come straight home and always ask before going to any of her friends' houses after school, but she hadn't taken much of a detour. Surely she wasn't all that late?

'I just walked a different way home, that's all. Down Cathays Terrace. It's not really out of my way.'

'Who were you with?'

'I walked a little way with Selina, only to the garage, then I turned off.'

'Why walk that way? I wish you'd stick to the way we always come. If I wanted you for something, I'd know where to find you then.'

'O.K.' Hannah breathed a sigh of relief because her mother hadn't insisted on an explanation. 'Why were you meeting me, anyway?'

'Tim's gone to his friend's house to tea and I came up to meet his mother—pass him over, sort of, so I thought I'd walk home with you.'

'Oh, I see.' Hannah fended off any more awkward questions by saying, 'I'm going upstairs to read the diary. I told you there's going to be a competition for the best project about the school, didn't I? There might be something I can use in it.'

'You can tidy your room while you're up there. It's a tip!'

Hannah flopped onto her bed and drew the diary out of her bag, once again thinking about her strange experience. Wouldn't it be wonderful if she could go back to Great-Gran's time for a whole day! Think of all she could write about then. There wasn't an awful lot about her schooldays in her diary: she'd had a much better glimpse of what it had been like in her—what had it been, a 'dream'? She would take it to school another day and try it out again. She had been actually holding the diary in her hands when she had visited the past, so perhaps the diary had special powers . . . Hannah's eyes were thoughtful as she wondered about the possibilities.

Nan rang the doorbell later that evening and Hannah opened the door to her.

'Hello, I wondered if you'd like to come for a little walk with me,' Nan said. 'I'm going to see a friend of mine. She hasn't been well and they gave me these flowers at the Church to take to her. D'you want to come? It's not far, just off Cathays Terrace—right across the road from where Great-Gran used to live.' Nan looked enquiringly at Hannah, a twinkle in her eyes.

'Oh, yes. I'll just ask Mum.' Hannah rushed through to the kitchen where her mother was stacking tins in the cupboards and Nan followed her.

'I asked Hannah if she would like to come with me to deliver these flowers,' Nan said. 'We won't be long.'

'Yes, sure.' Hannah's mother agreed. 'You don't have any homework, do you?'

Hannah shook her head, willing her mother not think of any reason why she shouldn't go and giving an excited whoop when she said, 'Yes.'

'Don't get so excited,' Nan said. 'You might find it a bit boring.'

'I won't be a moment, I'll just get my coat.' Hannah dashed upstairs and rummaged in her bag for the little velvet diary. She stuffed it in her pocket and ran back down to where Nan waited again.

The two women were talking about the bargains in the local supermarket and Hannah waited impatiently for them to finish, twisting her long hair around her finger until her mother told her to stop.

'You'd better brush it before you go out. Nan doesn't want to go out with a girl whose hair looks like rats' tails.'

Hannah went to the shelf where a hairbrush was kept for last-minute tidying up before school, and dragged it through her hair.

'There, that all right?' she asked. 'Can we go now?'

'Come on, then,' said Nan, 'before you burst with impatience. Won't be long,' she called over her shoulder to Hannah's mother.

'Thanks for asking me, Nan,' Hannah said, as they walked together. 'I looked to see if there was anyone I knew going this way on the way home today, but there was only Selina and she won't be friends with me.'

'Why not?' asked Nan. 'Although, I did tell you not to worry other people about it, didn't I?'

'I didn't get a chance to ask her. She hates me.'

'Why? What have you done to her?'

'Nothing. Some of the kids call her names, 'cos of the colour of her hair, you know it's red—and she's got a terrible temper.'

'I hope you don't do that!'

'I wouldn't dare! She'd kill me!'

Nan laughed. 'Anyway. This lady we're going to see was a friend of my mother's. She may have something to tell you.'

'Did she go to school with Great-Gran?'

'No, she's quite a bit younger than her. But she knew her very well. They were neighbours.'

'So she wouldn't have known her when she was my age?'

'No, but you wanted to see the sort of house

43

Great-Gran lived in, so now's your chance. She actually lived in that one over there.' Nan pointed across the road where the doorways of two houses came together.

Hannah felt a twinge of disappointment. Great-Gran's house was nowhere near the one they were to visit. But the diary might be useful.

'Oh, I see. I've brought the diary with me, just in case.'

Nan gave Hannah a puzzled glance and looked as if she was about to ask her something, but stopped at a red-painted front door, saying, 'This is it!' and rang the bell.

Hannah gazed at the long street of terraced houses with cars parked outside almost every door and tried to picture what it must have been like years ago.

An elderly lady opened the door, holding back a brown and white spaniel who tried to run out as soon as there was a wide enough space for him to get through.

'Behave yourself, Ben,' the lady scolded him. 'Come in, come in. He'll be all right as soon as the door's closed.'

'How are you, Mrs James?' Nan asked, as they followed the lady through a long passage. 'They gave me these flowers at the church to bring to you.'

'Oh, lovely. I'll just put them in water. Sit down. I won't be a minute. I've just brewed some tea.'

As the two grown-ups chatted, Hannah smoothed the dog, who was busily sniffing her skirt. Hannah guessed he could smell their cat on her. She looked around the room, which was not very big at all. She couldn't imagine a large family like Great-Gran's all fitting in.

A window looked out on to a stone wall that divided two houses and another door led through to Mrs James's kitchen. There were two armchairs, one each side of an electric fire that had three bars pouring out heat as if it were the middle of winter. In a corner of the room a television set talked to itself. Ben's toys lay in a wicker basket under the window and seeing Hannah looking at them, he brought a rubber bone to her and dropped it at her feet.

'Good boy!' she said, picking it up and tossing it across the room. The dog chased after it, almost knocking his mistress off her feet as she came in with a tray.

'Sorry,' Hannah said.

'Don't worry, love,' Mrs James said. 'He needs some exercise. I haven't been able to take him out, my back's been that bad.'

'I'll take him if you like,' Hannah said, eagerly. She had been trying to persuade her Dad to let her have a dog for ages, but he said it wouldn't get on with Oscar.

Mrs James looked at Hannah's Nan. 'Is that all right?'

'Just round the block then, and keep him on the lead so he won't run off.'

Mrs James fixed the lead to Ben's collar.

'There you are, son. This little girl's going to take you for nice walkies. Be a good boy!'

Hannah went out thankfully into the cool of the evening. She wondered how Mrs James could stand the heat in that room. It had been like a furnace! No wonder Ben was always trying to escape into the fresh air.

Hannah walked him sedately along the street, then looking back to make sure Nan wasn't watching from Mrs James's doorway, crossed the road and went back to stand outside the house that Nan said Great-Gran had lived in.

There was nothing to distinguish it from all the others in the street. She fingered the diary in her pocket—nothing. Perhaps she had fallen asleep for a moment in class after all.

She walked Ben around the block, stopping for him to sniff at every lamp-post on the way.

When she came back to the lamp-post on the corner by Mrs James's house, she was surprised to see that all the cars had gone, but clip-clopping along the street a solitary horse-drawn bread van was calling at houses. As she watched, the horse mounted the pavement and poked its head in at the doorway and refused to move until a woman gave it a sugar lump.

As she stood and gazed at this strange sight, Hannah suddenly found herself in the middle of a group of children playing on the corner. A girl in a plaid dress covered by a frilled pinafore swung round and round on a length of plaited yellow rope suspended from the arm of the lamp-post, narrowly missing Hannah as she swung out across the pavement. Another ran past her bowling a metal hoop, while some boys dressed just the way she had seen them in school, were playing a game.

Some of the boys had played it in the play-ground in her school—until it had been banned by Mr Harris who said it was too dangerous. It consisted of someone bending over with his hands around the waist of a boy who stood with his back against the wall while another boy jumped on to his back. The first one was then joined by another child holding on to his waist, who then had another person jumping on his back, and so it went on until eventually everyone collapsed on to the ground under the weight. And now here were these children playing it. Children who had lived eighty or more years ago!

Hannah watched, holding her breath in case she disturbed them. Then Ben barked, pulling against the lead until his eyes bulged, trying to drag her away from the corner. He was obviously terrified and wanted to get away from something he didn't understand. When Hannah looked back, the children had disappeared and everything was back as it was when she first entered the street.

Thinking about Ben's reaction later, Hannah realised that, on both times she had visited the past, she hadn't been afraid. But he was only a dog. He didn't understand that Great-Gran wouldn't hurt him.

As for Hannah herself, she couldn't stop smiling. It hadn't been a single day-dream in class after all. This new experience made her even more determined to see if she could get into Great-Gran's house. Think of all she might see if she managed that!

Chapter 5

When Nan opened Mrs James's front door in answer to Hannah's ring, Ben bolted inside and hid under a chair.

'What's the matter with you? Come on out!' Mrs James coaxed until Ben emerged, crawling along the carpet on his belly to cower at her feet and push his nose into her hand.

'What a silly boy you are. Hannah took you for a nice walk and now you're acting as if you're afraid of her!' She tickled him behind his ears and he began to sit up and behave in his usual doggie fashion.

'He's not used to going out with anyone else,' Mrs James apologised to Hannah. 'Did he behave himself?'

'Yes, he was fine. It was only when he got to the corner he began to pull on the lead. He wanted to get home to you again, I s'pose.' Hannah thought she couldn't very well tell his owner that he'd seen some ghostly children and was frightened.

Mrs James seemed satisfied by the explanation and began to make a fuss of Ben, obviously pleased to think that he preferred to be with her.

When his mistress walked to the front door with her visitors, Ben made no attempt to run out this time. Instead he hid behind Mrs James while she said goodbye to Hannah and her Nan and the last they heard was Mrs James heaping praise on Ben for 'being a good boy and not running off'.

'So . . . what was wrong with him?' Nan asked, as they set off up the street together.

'You'll never guess!' Hannah, who had been wondering whether to confide in Nan, found herself pouring out all she had seen.

'Ah, yes. I remember, children used to swing on lamp-posts like that when I was young. My mother always told me not to do it, though, because we could hurt ourselves if we banged into the post.'

'And perhaps she'd done it herself!' laughed Hannah. 'Like Mr Harris telling the boys not to play that game. He'd probably played it himself— that's how he knew it was dangerous.'

'Possibly,' Nan said, with a smile. 'Are you satisfied now you've seen Great-Gran's street? You didn't ask Mrs James any questions. You were too keen to take the dog out.'

'It was so hot in there, I couldn't wait to get outside. Like Ben! I'd still like to see inside Great-Gran's. Don't s'pose I'll be able to, though.'

'I don't know whether I should encourage you in this. What if you got stuck in the past? What would I tell your Mum and Dad? And I'm not so sure your interest lies in finding out about the school. You seem more keen on getting into her house!'

Hannah looked back over her shoulder at the house that Nan had pointed out as being Great-Gran's and as she did, who should come out of it but Selina.

'I don't believe it!' she said.

'What?' asked Nan.

'You know that girl I told you about, Selina?'

'Yes.'

'She's just come out of the house Great-Gran used to live in!'

'Oh, dear.' From the tone of her voice Nan sensed trouble brewing. 'If I were you I wouldn't say anything to her.'

Hannah was already wondering how she could get round Selina and wangle an invitation into her home, but the more she thought about it, the more impossible it seemed.

That night she wrote down all she had seen in the classroom and in the street and went to bed trying to think of a way she could see Selina's house. She dreamed of climbing over the wall into her garden, and dogs chasing her and trapping her in trees. She was glad to wake up and find everything normal.

Next day, she kept looking at Selina and wondering how she could mend the rift between them. But even when she stood next to her in lines, she couldn't think of anything to say.

After school, Hannah's mother was waiting for her outside the school gate.

'Tim's gone to play with his friend, Nathan, again,' she said. 'So I thought I'd wait and walk home with you.'

'Who's this friend, Nathan?' Hannah asked. 'I haven't heard about him before.'

'Oh, he hasn't been in Cardiff long, but they've become very friendly lately. Nathan's got quite a few Action Men. That's the attraction, I think. Anyway, it means I'll have to go and collect him after tea. Perhaps you'd like to walk down there with me?'

'Where do they live?'

If it was a long way, Hannah was going to refuse.

'Same street you went to with Nan last night.'

'Oh, yes, all right then.'

'Actually, he's got a sister in the same class as you. Now what was her name? Sally? Sarah? Something like that!'

'Not Selina!' Hannah exclaimed.

'Yes, that's right. Her mother was telling me that she's not very happy there. The children pick on her. I hope you're not one of them.'

'The children pick on *her*!' Hannah was indignant.

'You should see her! She's really nasty. You can't say a word to her without her flying into a temper. And I don't pick on her—I keep out of her way.'

'Well, some people must, because her mother says she sometimes goes home in tears.'

'Some kids call her "Carrots" and "Ginger", but she gives as good as she gets.'

'Well, try and be nice to her; she's probably prickly because she's unhappy.'

Some chance, thought Hannah. If I was nice to her, she'd think I was making fun of her or something. Still, Selina or no Selina, she would have a chance tonight to have a glimpse of Great-Gran's old home.

At half-past six that evening Hannah and her mother set off to pick up Tim. Tucked safely in Hannah's pocket was Great-Gran's diary, just in case.

Selina's front door had a black knocker in the shape of a lion's head and when her mother lifted it to knock, Hannah half expected it to roar.

Selina's mother had red hair just like her daughter's, but unlike Selina, she welcomed them in with a smile.

Great-Gran's house had been modernised up to the hilt, like most of the small terraced houses. Radiators stood against walls and spot lights aimed at them from ceilings. No need for cleaning out ashes or candles to light you to bed now. Hannah realised she had been expecting to see it all as it once was.

'I've just told them to pick up their toys. I knew you'd be along soon.'

'Has he been good?'

'Oh, yes. They've really enjoyed themselves. It's so nice that Nathan's found a friend. I wish I could say the same for Selina. She mopes around all on her own,' Selina's mother sighed.

'Oh, by the way, this is my daughter, Hannah. It appears she's in the same class as your Selina.'

Mrs Grantham looked with interest at Hannah as if sizing her up to see if she would make a suitable friend for her unhappy daughter. Hannah had the feeling that at any moment someone was going to suggest her taking Selina under her wing at school and she was cringing at the thought.

Before anyone could say a word, however, Selina came into the room and glared at Hannah.

Mrs Grantham said, 'Hullo love. Look who's here! Did you know that Hannah is Tim's sister? She's in your class, I understand.'

'Yeah,' Selina said, gruffly.

Mrs Grantham raised an eyebrow at Hannah's mother and said no more.

Nathan and Tim finished packing up the toys,

they said goodbye to Mrs Grantham and the children and began to walk back home.

'Your friend's not very chatty, is she?'

'She's not my friend, I told you,' Hannah replied.

'Well, you could make an effort and try to get to know her—you might like her then. Perhaps she is unhappy, like her mother says.'

'I'd rather make friends with . . .' Hannah sought her worst nightmare and said, '. . . a boa constrictor!'

'Oh, dear!' Her mother looked thoughtful but didn't try to persuade her.

Hannah knew she hadn't heard the last of it, however. Her mother was like a dog worrying a bone when she had an idea in her head.

'Why don't you like her?' asked Tim. 'She's all right. Although she did scream at Nathan when he used her Barbie caravan to put his Action men in.'

'So would Hannah if you did that to her.'

'Yes, I would,' said Hannah. 'But she screams at everybody about everything. I wouldn't say she's all right!'

Hannah fingered the diary in her pocket. No sign of the ghostly children today. Perhaps Selina's house had been changed too much and they didn't feel at home there any more.

Chapter 6

'. . . I went to Selina's house with Mum to fetch Tim, but I didn't see anything. There was nothing there.'

Hannah had decided to confide in her best friend about the things she had seen when she held the diary, but Laura was looking at her in a funny way, as if not quite sure whether she was joking or not.

A voice broke in on their conversation. 'So you came to spy on us, did you? I might have known. I wondered what you were up to. Teacher's pet!'

Hannah spun round to see Selina standing, hands on her hips, glaring at her.

'I d-didn't,' she stammered. 'We came to get Tim. You know that!'

'That's not what you were just saying to your friend there,' Selina spat the words at her.

Hannah knew she'd have to offer some sort of explanation. She didn't know just how much Selina had heard.

'My Great-Gran used to live in your house when she was a girl.'

'So! Is that any reason to come spying on us?'

'I told you, we came to fetch Tim.'

'And to have a good nosey round. I heard you

say you didn't see anything, that there was nothing there! We're not good enough for you, I suppose!'

'Oh, what's the point? Leave her alone.' Laura tugged at Hannah's arm, trying to pull her away.

'Why did you call me "teacher's pet"? I'm not!'

Hannah seized on the words to try and divert Selina's attention from her visit the night before.

'Because you are! You and your Grannie's diary. I bet you made it up yourself.'

Hannah shrugged. 'If that's what you want to believe. I don't care.'

'It's not fair. You've got all sorts of things in it that we don't know, so you're bound to win the prize.'

'Make up your mind,' Laura said. 'One minute you're saying Hannah made up what's in the diary and then you say she'll win because she knows more about it than the rest of us. You can't have it both ways.'

Selina stormed off, her red hair bouncing on her shoulders as she went.

Laura and Hannah stared at each other in amazement.

'What brought that on?' Laura said.

'She overheard what I was saying and got it all wrong.'

Hannah felt thoroughly miserable. She had sounded like a real gossip to Selina just now and had clearly made matters even worse between them.

That day Mr Harris announced details of the competition.

'So that you will each have the same opportunity, I have given your teachers some folders. It's up to you how you fill them. You can use pictures and drawings and if there is anyone who hasn't a computer of their own for the written work, see me and I'll work out a rota for you to use the school ones.'

The best part of it was the prizes. There were to be two prizes, one for the seven to eight year olds and another for the nines to elevens.

'Let's see how original and decorative you can make them,' said Mr Harris, then added cheerfully, 'Good luck!'

During the English lesson, Miss Edwards gave out the folders. They had black, stiff cardboard covers with punched holes at the sides threaded with laces so that additional pages could be added if all the ones supplied were used up.

'How can we write on black, Miss?' Tom Carter put his hand up. 'Nothing will show up.'

'Any ideas?' Miss Edwards looked around the class with a smile.

'Put a label on the front?' Laura suggested.

'White crayon or paint?' Hannah said.

'What's the point in doing anything? She's going to win.' Selina pointed at Hannah.

'That's not the right attitude,' Miss Edwards said. 'If you don't try, you won't stand a chance, will you? I'm sure if you look around to find some old books or go to the Local Studies place in the library, you'll all find something of interest—and original!'

Hannah stole a glance at Selina. She was staring out through the window, looking bored on purpose. She must be sulking, thought Hannah.

Now, I suggest that today you make a start by selecting a title for your project and thinking of a way to decorate the cover. Tom, if you will fetch the paints off the shelf, we'll begin—but be careful with them. Don't spill them!'

Hannah chewed on her pencil for a while, wondering what would make the most dramatic cover for her work. A picture of the school in the centre? With, perhaps, some drawing or pictures of various things used over the years. She began to sketch a cover on a piece of rough paper. She made a half circle with the letters made up out of the school's name and underneath printed 1900—2000. There could be graphics of old school desks, a cane hanging on the blackboard, a boy sitting in the corner with a dunce's cap on his head . . .

She was so engrossed in her work, she didn't

notice, until Miss Edwards raised her voice chiding William for being careless, that one of the boys had spilt a pot of white poster paint over the table he was working on and several children were trying to wipe up the thick paint.

Hannah went over to help, putting some paper towels on the floor to catch any drips.

'Someone bring over that black bag, will you please?' Miss Edwards nodded towards the rubbish bag the caretaker had left in a corner especially for messy art lessons.

Tom ran to get it, then held it open for the paint-soaked paper towels to be put in. William decided at that moment to scoop the remaining paint towards the side of the table and it dribbled all down the side of the bag.

'For goodness' sake, William. Don't make any more mess! You are a thoughtless boy! Just throw all the papers in the bag and I'll put it behind the blackboard for Mr Miles to take away later. The rest of you sit down and get on with your work while I fetch a wet cloth and clear up this mess. The ones on this table will have to sit somewhere else for the time being.'

The small crisis over, Hannah sat down and went on with her drawing. She'd ask Mum if she had any of the graphics she needed on disk when she went home.

Seeing Nan working in her front garden on the way home, she decided to pop over to tell her about her visit to Selina's house.

'Hello, is it half-past three already?' Nan asked.

'Quarter to four, actually.'

'Where does the time go? Have you been home? Would you like a glass of lemonade?'

'Better not, thanks. Mum'll wonder where I am. I just wanted to tell you that I went to Great-Gran's old house last night. No luck, though.'

'Good gracious! How did you manage that?'

'Well, it turned out that Tim is friendly with Selina's brother. Remember? We saw her coming out of her house when we went to see Mrs James. Me and Mum went to collect Tim after tea.'

'No ghostly children hanging about this time?'

Hannah had the impression that Nan was teasing her and said huffily, 'I thought you believed me!'

'I'm sure you must have seen something. You wouldn't say you had otherwise.'

Slightly mollified, Hannah said, 'I think the house has been modernised too much. Great-Gran wouldn't feel at home there. It's nothing like it would have been when she was young.'

'Of course, Selina's house was the one Great-Gran lived in when she was married. She lived next door when she was a girl.'

Hannah looked at her grandmother in surprise.

'I didn't know that! Why didn't you tell me?'

'I don't know. Perhaps I thought you knew already.'

'Well, I didn't. That makes everything different, doesn't it?'

'I don't see why.'

'Because the diary is all about her as a girl, and when I have the diary with me and it's in a place she used to live in—or in her school, it's then she appears! I wonder who lives in that house . . . What number is it?'

'The front doors of Selina's house and the one you want are side by side. I don't know who lives there now. Mrs James would know.

'You see, what happened, was that shortly after Great-Gran was married, the house next door to her mother became vacant and she and my father moved in there. They stayed there until her parents died and then they moved away.'

But Hannah wasn't listening. Her mind was full of the new information Nan had given her. It made all the difference. Now all she had to do was find out who lived next door to Selina and see if it was someone she knew—and perhaps be invited in. Maybe, even if she stood by the front door she might have some luck.

Chapter 7

'Mum! Have you got any graphics I could use on the cover of my project?'

'What kind of thing d'you want?'

'Something about school, but old-fashioned. The sort of things they'd have used when the school first opened.'

'I'll have a look. I think there's a quill pen in an ink-pot, a teacher with a cane . . . Will that do?'

'That'd be great. Although, they wouldn't write with a quill, it would have been a nib with a wooden handle. Anyway, can you see what you've got and print them off for me?'

'I'll do it tonight. I'm busy at the moment. Is that O.K.?'

'Yes, thanks.' Hannah agreed, absentmindedly, still thinking about what Nan had told her. 'Did you know that Great-Gran lived next door to her mother when she married?'

Her mother thought for a moment, 'I can't remember having heard that, but perhaps I've forgotten. I expect Dad would know.'

Hannah went upstairs to finish planning her cover. Opening her bag, she felt inside for the paper on which she had started her drawing. Her fingers failed to find it. Opening the top wider, she saw it and began to pull it out—but there seemed to be something missing, the bag wasn't full enough. Then she realised! The diary wasn't there.

Searching through the books, pencil case and papers, she still couldn't find it. Quickly, she tipped everything out on her bed. It definitely wasn't there.

For a moment it seemed as if the world stood still. She'd lost Great-Gran's diary! But how could she have? She was sure she had taken it out of her pocket after going to Selina's house.

Her pocket! That's where it would be. She must have been mistaken about taking it out.

Hannah searched her jacket pockets, first one, then the other and then went back and looked again. Was this the coat she had had on?

Looking through every coat and jacket in her wardrobe, she became more frantic with each failure to find the small book. Surely it hadn't fallen out last night when she went to Selina's house: she would have felt it drop—or heard it.

Had her mother borrowed it for some reason and forgotten to tell her? But Hannah was afraid to ask: Mum had told her she shouldn't take it to school in case she lost it. But she had been so sure that that wouldn't happen. And what would Nan say?

Hannah was very quiet at the table that night, so quiet that her mother asked. 'You all right, love?'

'Yes, fine!' she said in a too-bright voice, wondering what would happen if she confessed now. Mum and Dad were always telling her off for losing things. Like the time Mum had lent her that little ring to wear and she'd left it on the basin in dancing class when she'd taken it off to wash her hands. And when Dad had given her that thing for making circles . . . 'Your bedroom's like a black hole: anything that goes in there vanishes for ever!' Dad's words came back to her making her determined not to tell them. She'd have a look in school first, because perhaps she'd dropped it there. She was certain by now that she had taken it out of her pocket and put it back in her school bag last night.

That night Hannah couldn't get to sleep. She turned from side to side trying to find a comfortable position, but it seemed as if the mattress had developed ridges during the day and sheets wrapped themselves round her in a tangle as if they were trying to hold her down.

She must have dozed, because the room was dark when she opened her eyes again, except for a kind of glow coming from the corner of her room.

Her first thought was that it was her mother, the electric night light illuminating her white dressing gown and making it glow. Her mother always looked in on her and on Tim in his room before going to bed herself.

But when Hannah's eyes became accustomed to the dark, she began to make out the figure of a young girl. She was dressed in a white frock and frilled picture hat and in her hand she held a spray of flowers. With a shock, Hannah recognised her. It was Great-Gran—dressed as she had described herself when having her photograph taken! Had she come to tell her how cross she was because Hannah had lost her diary?

But the girl seemed to be pointing to something. Something dark standing in the corner. It was a bag, a black rubbish bag with a stream of white stuff running down the side of it.

Hannah's mind went back to the classroom, to the children around the table and Tom scooping the tipped paint over the edge of the table on to the black bag! Did this mean that Great-Gran knew where her diary was? But how had it got there?

Selina!

'Oh, thank you. Thank you very much. I'm sorry I didn't take more care of your diary. I won't take it to school again—if I can only get it back.'

The girl smiled and as Hannah stared, she

seemed to fade away into the darkest corner of her room. Hannah blinked and rubbed her eyes, but the girl had gone.

She lay back on her pillows and wondered about what she'd seen. At least Great-Gran in her vision hadn't been cross with her, but had seemed to be showing her where her diary was. Hannah felt hopeful now about getting it back. But what a strange thing it was to be helped by a ghost!

Hannah made up her mind to go to school early the next morning and see if Mr Miles had taken the bag away.

She slept then, waking only when she heard Tim racing along the landing playing at aeroplanes. For once, she was glad of his noise in the morning because it meant she could leave early and find Mr Miles before anyone else arrived.

'So you're not walking to school with us this morning?' her mother asked, when Hannah said she would have to leave early.

'No, there's something I have to do before school starts. Something for the project,' she said, when her mother opened her mouth to protest.

'You'll want these then,' Hannah's mother went to her desk and picked up some papers. 'I ran those graphics off for you last night.'

'Thanks, Mum.' Hannah pushed them in her bag. 'Bye!'

She hurried up the road as fast as she could and, turning through the gates, saw Mr Miles walking across the playground carrying a black rubbish bag in each hand and she looked eagerly to see if there were white paint marks on the sides.

'Hello! You're early this morning. Couldn't you sleep?'

'I lost a book yesterday and I think it might have been put in the black bag with the rubbish. Have you done ours yet?'

'What class are you in?'

'6E.' Hannah waited, not breathing, for his answer.

'Oh, yes. I did that last night.'

'It hasn't gone to the tip, has it?' Hannah said, expecting the worst.

'No-o. Not yet. The men haven't been yet. It'll be over there on that trolley.'

Hannah looked to where he pointed and saw under cover of the sheds, a tall metal cage, almost full to the top with black bags.

She'd never find it amongst that lot! But if the paint mark was facing outwards she'd be all right. Walking round the trolley, she looked up and down the stacked bags searching for some sign of the one she needed so desperately. She had almost completed the circuit when she saw it, lying on its side, with its give-away mark showing.

'That's it!' she said, poking it to show Mr Miles.

'Thank goodness it's not one of the bottom ones,' he said, beginning to lift off the top ones.

A small group of children had gathered by this time and amongst them was Laura.

'What's up?' she asked.

'I lost my diary,' Hannah said, 'and I'm pretty sure it was put in with the rubbish yesterday.'

'What makes you think that?' Laura was looking at her in a strange way.

'Tell you later. Help me have a look, will you?'

Mr Miles handed the waste bag over to Hannah.

'Mind you put it all back after you,' he said.

Hannah promised she would and without hesitation opened it up and began to feel around inside.

She shook her head. 'It's no good, we're going to have to tip it all out.' Without more ado, she up-ended the sack and tipped papers, bits of card and pencil shavings all out on to the ground.

'There it is!' Hannah dived into the rubbish, bringing out her treasured book. She kissed it and put it safely in her bag. Then she looked with dismay at the rubbish.

'I'd like to get my hands on the person who did it,' she muttered. Then, turning to Laura she said, 'See if Mr Miles will give you a brush to clear this lot up, will you? I'll go on putting the paper back in.'

Laura went off and Hannah began her task.

'Good Heavens!' drawled a voice. 'You practising for when you leave school? You gonna be a bin man?'

Hannah looked up to see Selina smirking at her.

'You wouldn't know anything about this, would you?' she demanded. 'I can't think of anyone else mean enough to do it.'

'What? Tip the rubbish out on to the playground for you to pick up?'

'You know what I'm talking about! Putting my diary in with the rubbish yesterday!'

'Why would I do a thing like that?' mocked Selina.

'Because you're jealous, that's why. You said yesterday it wasn't fair that I had it, so you decided to get rid of it.'

Selina coloured and turned away.

Laura came up with a brush and pan just then.

'What's going on?' she asked.

'Oh, she's trying to be funny. But who else would put it there? I'd have lost it for good if . . .' Hannah stopped. She'd been about to say, 'Great-Gran hadn't shown me where it was,' but she knew even Laura wouldn't believe that. 'I just know, that's all!'

Selina gave them a pitying glance and then walked off, her nose in the air.

Laura held the dustpan while Hannah swept the small pieces of rubbish into it. Then they tied the bag again and together threw it on top of the heap.

'Have you put it away safe now?' Laura asked. 'I wouldn't want to do that again.'

Hannah patted her bag, feeling the hard corners of the book through it. 'I won't bring it again,' she said. 'I thought it was gone for good—and I'm not really supposed to carry it with me.'

'Why did you do it then?' Laura's tone was sharp. 'Selina thinks you did it to show off.'

Hannah gave her friend a puzzled look. How could she think a thing like that? But there was no time to argue now, the playground was empty and all the other children had already marched into school.

As they entered the gloom of the lobby and hung up their coats, Hannah glanced back towards a dark corner. Just for a second she saw Great-Gran, dressed in her everyday clothes now. As Hannah looked at her, Great-Gran gave her a warm smile of approval, then disappeared.

Chapter 8

'Come along, girls! Where have you been? I saw you in the playground half an hour ago. What have you been doing?'

Miss Edwards looked cross, her fingers rapping a tattoo on the table as she waited for their excuses.

'It's not our fault, Miss Edwards. Someone threw my diary in the bin bag yesterday and we had to tip everything out to find it and then sweep it all back up again.'

'What do you mean, "someone threw it in there." Who would do such a thing?'

Hannah glanced at Selina, who was staring at the table top as if something of vital importance were there.

'Well? Did you see someone do it?'

'No, Miss.'

'Then how do you know it wasn't picked up with other papers accidentally and thrown away?'

Hannah could see the logic of her teacher's argument, but . . .

'It wasn't on my desk, Miss Edwards. It was in my bag.'

'Are you sure?'

'Yes, Miss.'

Miss Edwards frowned. 'Does anyone know anything about this?'

No one spoke.

'How did you know where to find it?'

Hannah had been dreading this question, knowing that no one would believe her if she told them the truth.

'I tried to think of all the places it could be, and I remembered the rubbish bag we used yesterday.'

'So there were no grounds for saying that "someone threw it in there"?'

'Well, I certainly didn't put it in there, Miss Edwards,' Hannah said.

'Neither did I,'

'Nor me, Miss.'

'I didn't, Miss.'

Denials came from all parts of the classroom.

'That's enough. We've wasted too much time already on this business. You must not make wild accusations if you haven't any grounds for doing so. It was probably carelessness on your part, Hannah. You always seem to be losing something. Now! All of you get out your books and turn to page 103.'

Hannah seethed inwardly. Selina was getting off scot-free and it wasn't fair, but she wouldn't get her hands on the diary ever again, Hannah would make sure of that.

There was another surprise in store for Hannah that day. As she walked home from school in the afternoon, she saw Nan waiting at her gate.

'Hello. I hoped I'd see you. Has Mr Harris said anything to you about me coming to speak to the children at school?'

'No. What does he want you to talk about?'

'We-ell. You know this project for the school's Centenary?' Hannah nodded. 'He thought it would be nice if I went up and told the Juniors what it was like when I was there.'

'Oh!' Hannah thought for a moment, not quite sure what she thought about this news. 'Will you be coming to our class?'

'I should think so. I hope he doesn't want me to stand up in front of the whole school; I don't think I could do that. One class at a time would be all right, though.'

Hannah felt a bit put out. She'd hoped to keep all the information people in her family could give her to herself. Now everyone would know as much as she did and her chance of winning the prize dwindled.

'It's only fair, isn't it?' Nan said. 'It wouldn't be right if I told only you. As it is, you've got Great-Gran's diary.'

'Mmm, but Miss Edwards read out parts of that to the class.'

In spite of Nan's words, Hannah would have liked to keep it all a secret, only to spring it on the school at the very end when her project would be chosen as the best and she would win the CD player.

But then a thought occurred to her. There was still the diary's special power. Perhaps it would reveal other things to her that were not written down.

She smiled at Nan.

'Yes, I suppose it wouldn't be really fair. Wait 'til I tell Laura you're coming to talk to us! She'll be surprised.'

Hannah went home and told her mother Nan's news.

'Yes, I know,' she said. 'Actually, Mr Harris asked me at the Parents'/Teachers' meeting if I thought Nan would do it, but I said he would have to ask her himself. Actually, she seems quite keen on the idea. She did wonder, though, what you thought. If you'd mind her coming.'

'Of course I don't mind. Why should I?' Hannah pushed any selfish thoughts about keeping everything for herself to the back of her mind.

'That's all right then. She's going to see Mr Harris tomorrow, to work out a suitable time.'

Hannah's class were filing into the Hall for choir practice the following day just as Nan came through the lobby and turned up the stairs to Mr Harris's office.

'What's your Nan doing here?' hissed Laura. 'You didn't tell her Selina took the diary, did you?'

'No.' Hannah explained Nan's mission.

'Oh, good. Now you won't be the only pebble on the beach, will you?'

Hannah was surprised at Laura's words, but thinking about it, she supposed Laura must have been feeling a teeny bit jealous of all the attention she was getting.

'That's what Mum said. That it would be better to share what she knows with everybody.'

'You didn't offer to share what's in the diary with me, though, did you?'

'I told you about it and you didn't want to know. Said it wasn't as interesting as your Disney collection!'

'Yes, but that was before I knew about the competition!'

'Girls! Quiet now. We're ready to start.'

Miss Davies settled herself at the piano and began to play the introduction while Miss Edwards stood in front to conduct, but all the way through the singing lesson Hannah pondered on Laura's words. She supposed she had been selfish not sharing with her best friend. Laura seemed to think so; had been quite huffy about it in fact. Should she offer to show Laura the diary now? Perhaps that would make amends. First she would finish reading it herself.

Nov. 11th.

Saw a lot of soldiers marching down Cathays Terrace from the Army Barracks today. They were very smart in their khaki uniforms and puttees. Someone said they were parading to the General Station before being shipped over to France. I hope they all keep safe, but I suppose that's impossible; some are bound to be hurt. It's been very dark today, with black clouds making it seem like dusk all day. We could hardly see to write in class in the middle of the afternoon, so the gas lights had to be lit.

Dec. 14th.

We heard that Albany Road School has been opened as an emergency hospital. There have been so many men injured in France that the Infirmary can't cope. The children who go Albany have to share with Marlborough Road School.

One school uses it in the morning, the other one in the afternoon. Why didn't they use Gladstone? We'd only have school for half a day then.

Feb. 1915.
Found my diary at last, but Emma had ripped some pages out of it to draw on. I'll hide it from her in future, but it's difficult when we all share the same bedroom.

Feb. 7th.
Mama had Margaret's photograph taken for her seventh birthday. She had on her new tartan dress with a frilled white pinafore covering it. Mama had put curling rags in the night before and her hair hung in ringlets over her shoulders for the photograph. Mrs Thomas bought her some new button boots. Margaret's always been her favourite.

Feb. 14th.

Miss Davies said that I'm to have a part in the St. David's Day concert. The only problem is that I must have a herald's costume. I asked Mama and she said she'll see what she can do.

Feb. 20th.

Mama found that the gas mantle was broken when she tried to light the gas, so she sent me to Warman's to buy a new one. On the way I met Frank who told me that he is going in the Army. I shall miss him because he often carries the washing basket for me when he sees it's really heavy. He promised to write to me when he goes. I don't think Mama will be cross if he does.

Feb. 29th.

Mama made a tunic for my part as Herald out of an old coat. She said she sat up sewing half the night to finish it.

It looks quite smart, although I think it would have been better in a bright red. Brown is a bit drab.

March 1st.

At last St. David's Day has come. Yesterday Miss Hemmings said that if our mothers and fathers wanted to come and see the concert the school would need extra chairs, so she asked anyone who was able to bring a wooden kitchen chair with them. We had to write our names in chalk on the bottom so they wouldn't get mixed up. It was so funny to walk up Cathays Terrace and see a lot of children struggling with their chairs. Some of them even turned them upside down and carried them on their heads!

The concert went off well. We sang 'God bless the Prince of Wales' and a Welsh lullaby when the baby was born. I didn't forget my part, although I was afraid I might. When I looked at Mama, she was smiling as if she was pleased with me.

March 12th.
Frank has gone. He came to say goodbye to us before he left. Mama had tears in her eyes—although she said she wasn't crying. She pretended she had something in her eye. I went with Frank to the front door when he left and I asked him if he had meant it when he said he would write to me. He said, 'Yes' and gave me a kiss. I was so happy, I asked him if he would wait for me to grow up so we could get married. He smiled, but looked sad at the same time, and said, 'I wouldn't have anyone else'. When he walked away, I felt like crying too.

March 15th.
Caught Lillian reading my diary. I am going to find a place to hide it. Mama

gave me a beautiful sewing box which had been her mother's. It is made of rosewood and has an inlaid design on the top. There's even a key. I think I shall put my diary on the bottom and cover it with sewing things; Lillian's not likely to use those and I shall know it's safe from prying eyes. Not that there is anything in it I would be ashamed of anyone reading, but it's private and she shouldn't look.

March 17th.
We took Emma to Sunday School for the first time. It was a lovely sunny day, so Mama let her come with us. We showed her how to push her Star Card through the little window to get it stamped and told her about getting a prize if she comes every week. She had to go in the Beginners' Class on her own and she cried, but she soon settled down when we reminded her about the prize.

Whitsun.

We all went to the Whitsun Treat, marching down to Queen Street Station with the Boys' Brigade Band parading in front of us, playing their instruments. The sound of the music made me feel very excited. No wonder they play music for soldiers to march to — it probably helps them on their way to the Front. We caught the train to the field and as we arrived we were each given a glass of milk and a big currant bun. There were swings and a slide and coconut shies. Later on there were races with a prize for the winner of each race. I couldn't run fast enough, but we had a good time.

August Bank Holiday.

I'm not going to write in my diary every day: the pages will last longer if I only write down important things and it's silly to write down 'Nothing happened', so often.

Today Mama took us all to Roath Park. Sidney was in the pram , while Emma sat on a board across the top. We took sandwiches, a kettle and everything we needed to make a cup of tea. We walked across the Prom to see where they're building the memorial to Captain Scott. I don't know why they decided to build a lighthouse. I suppose it was because he was a sea captain. The foundations went down an awfully long way. Mama said we will come back another day to see how they are getting on.

We stopped on the Lake Road West side of the park and played on the grass for a while. Then Mama filled the kettle with water, and after putting a penny in the slot, lit one of the big gas stoves to boil the water. It's funny how much nicer bread and jam tastes when you are out in the open. Fairoak Road hill seemed very steep on the way back, but we all helped push the pram which made it easier.

Sept. 20th.
My birthday. I only remembered my diary when someone reminded me about having it from Auntie Lizzie last year. That's the trouble with hiding it under the things in my sewing box: I tend to forget all about it. Mama took me to have my photograph taken in town. I had on my new white dress and the man made me pose with a spray of flowers. I sat on a stool in the middle of the studio and he told me to look dreamy. It was difficult to sit still while he did things with the camera and my face started to twitch. It always does that when I'm in front of a camera.

Sept. 25th.
Mama had my photograph back from Jerome's today. It was very nice, although

I didn't think it was really like me.
Mama likes it though, and said she is
going to send one to her sister in Neath.

Oct. 31st.
No Bob-Apple Party this year as Mama
didn't have many apples from her
cousin in Somerset. Dada's thinking
about taking an allotment. He had a
leaflet from the Corporation asking
people to grow their own food and
giving a list of the parks which were
going to be divided up into plots. He's
putting his name down for one in
Llandaff Fields. It'll save having to
traipse out to Mam's cousin in Ely
to swop our butter for their fresh
vegetables — it would be nice to have a
bit of butter for ourselves too. One day,
when I'm grown up I'm going to marry
a rich man and I'll have butter on my
bread every day! I just hope the war
will be over by then.

Nov. 25th.

It's awful to see the wounded men who are being looked after in Albany Road School. Some have bandages over their eyes and are led along by others; some are wheeled in bath chairs because they have lost a leg. I wonder how Frank is getting along. I hope he is safe.

Dec. 15th.

Mama heard they were having margarine in the Maypole today, so she sent Margaret and Emma along to stand in the queue. When they heard they could only have half a pound, they stood in different places because half a pound would not go far between nine of us. They had to smile when some ladies in the queue said, 'Don't those two girls look alike? They could be sisters.' Of course, they thought that was very funny, but they had to try not to laugh.

Dec. 20th.

Nearly Christmas. Everyone had a present from school today. The older ones like me had a book of tables and the little ones had a piece of paper which, when the corner was lit, burnt out a picture. I don't know how it works and when I asked Dada, he didn't know either although he pretended he did, but said it would be too difficult for me to understand.

Jan. 14th, 1916.

They said the war would be over by that first Christmas, but it still drags on and more and more schools are being opened to take care of the wounded. Len has joined the Voluntary Aid Detachment and is helping with the wounded in Albany Road School. He said if they won't have him in the army until he's seventeen, he can do some good until he's old enough to go.

Feb. 8th.

Mama heard they were having potatoes in on Kingsway today, so she kept me home from school so I could stand in the queue. The end of the line was near the New Theatre when I first got there and it went all along The Friary and over Kingsway. It's bitterly cold today: the wind coming up Kingsway past the Castle was enough to cut you in two. A lazy wind Mam calls it: it would rather go through you than round you. My hands and feet were like blocks of ice by the time I got near the shop. Mama had given me the canvas frail and told me to get as many as I could, but when I was almost at the shop, the man came out and said 'Sold out!' I cried a bit on the way back up Park Place lane — what with the cold and disappointment — and I knew Mama would be upset too. It's difficult for her to make the food go round.

Feb. 15th.

We're learning a new Welsh song in school for St. David's Day and Lillian is nearly driving us all mad singing 'Hob y deri dando' over and over again. I told her she should learn the rest of it or be quiet.

Chapter 9

Nan came to the school on Wednesday afternoon the following week. She had confessed to Hannah that she felt a bit nervous.

'What if they don't listen to me?' she said. 'What if I can't make it interesting enough?'

'Just tell them the way you told me. I was interested, wasn't I? And they all want to win the prize. If they don't listen, they won't be able to write about what you tell them.'

'I suppose you're right,' agreed Nan and seemed much more cheerful after that.

When Nan came into Hannah's classroom, she had already been in the school for an hour, had told what she could remember of her schooldays to several classes and seemed to be quite at ease.

First, Miss Edwards introduced her, although she didn't tell everyone that their visitor was Hannah's grandmother. She just said that Nan was going to tell them what the school was like when she was a girl.

As the teacher had been speaking, Nan had been looking around the classroom—at the walls, the tables and the children themselves.

'I'd like to say how clever you all are to be able

to make all those little houses and the pictures you've decorated the school with. We didn't do anything like that when I was here, I'm afraid. The only handiwork we did was needlework on a Friday afternoon.'

'Did the boys do needlework too?' David Hughes giggled as he asked the question.

Nan smiled. 'We didn't have boys in our class. This part of the school, downstairs that is, was for girls only. The boys were upstairs.'

David's face was a study as he sat back down. 'Cor, they were lucky, not having to put up with stupid girls!'

'The boys and girls were kept apart in those days. Even the playground was divided. There was a high wall built from the sheds to the Junior school doorway. And we didn't have indoor toilets then, either. We had to run across the playground in all kinds of weather. The cookery school was built on the girls' side of the playground—where the Nursery school is now—and the boys' carpentry building on their side.'

'Carpentry? The boys did carpentry? What did they make?' Tom was interested now.

'I don't really know. You see, only the boys and girls who didn't pass the High School exam went to those classes. I suppose it was to prepare them for when they left school at fourteen.'

'They left school at fourteen? Lucky dabs!' Tom grinned at Miss Edwards as he said this.

'Did you pass the High School exam?'

'Yes,' said Nan. 'Although I didn't expect to. Our teacher, Miss Taylor, told us that she'd take us all for a walk to see the outside of the High School because we'd never see the inside of it!'

Nan grinned. 'I don't know whether she said it to make us work harder, but I remember that most of the class passed. I don't know whether that was a surprise to her, or if she really knew that we had it in us and didn't want us to feel nervous. But anyway, she must have been pleased to know that we'd done well.'

Nan went on to tell them about the kind of lessons she'd had until Tom asked whether she'd ever had the cane.

Miss Edwards explained, 'They all went to St. Fagans recently and saw the old schoolhouse there. They had to sit up straight in the desks with their arms crossed and Mr Thomas marched up and down in front of the class shouting at them and threatening them with the cane. They haven't forgotten that!'

Nan laughed. 'Well, some children had the cane if they were naughty. But most of them were quite well-behaved. The teachers were very strict and made sure of that. One teacher, Miss Davies, well, she only had to walk into the room and everyone would sit still and be quiet. I remember, she was a very large lady with hair scraped back into a bun. We were all dead scared of her!'

'Did you learn Welsh?' Rhian, whose family was Welsh and spoke the language fluently, asked.

'Yes, a bit. We learnt Welsh songs and some phrases, the days of the week and the months, things like that.'

'When we went to St. Fagans they told us that when children went to that school they were not allowed to speak Welsh. If they did, they had "Welsh Not" written on a board that the teacher hung round their necks to remind them to speak English. They could only take it off when the next one spoke in Welsh, then they had to put it on.'

'That's very interesting, but I hadn't heard about that. That wasn't in my time at school at all.'

'Did you play hockey and lacrosse?' Laura was keen on these games herself.

'No, I'm afraid not. I can't remember playing any games, except the ones we played at playtime. We did exercises, touching our toes that sort of thing, and drill. Oh, and I vaguely remember taking part in a relay race.'

'Drill? What's drill?' Jonathan wanted to know.

'The sort of thing soldiers do, you know. March up and down. Obey commands. The space was limited you see.'

'Didn't you have music and movement?'

'No, I'm afraid not. We didn't have radios in school in those days.'

'No radio! What about television?'

Selina rounded on Tom, 'Don't be silly. They weren't invented then!'

Nan went on to describe the kind of lessons they'd had, how everyone did the same thing at the same time, not like the present day when individual tables could be working on different projects. Eventually, she glanced at her watch and saw that it was time to move on to the next class.

Before she left, Miss Edwards said, 'Thank you very much for coming to speak to us. I'm sure all the children will have learnt something today that they can put in their projects. If you like, we'll show you what they've written when they've finished.'

Nan said, 'Oh yes, I'd like that.' Then, saying a cheery goodbye and flashing a special smile at Hannah, she went on to the last class.

Selina fell into step with Hannah as they left the classroom.

'That was nice of your Gran to come and tell us what it was like when she was here,' she said.

Hannah was so surprised by this overture that she stammered as she replied, 'Oh, it was Mr

Harris's idea. Miss Edwards showed him Great-Gran's diary and he asked Nan if she'd come and tell everyone about the time she was in school.'

'It was nice of her, all the same. I didn't have a clue what to write before. Now I've got a better idea.' And with a half smile, Selina walked off across the playground on her own.

'What was Ginger saying to you?' Laura asked, as she caught up with Hannah.

'Nothing much.' Laura's reference to the colour of Selina's hair irritated Hannah. She had been feeling quite pleased that Selina had spoken to her. For once, she had been quite friendly. Now Laura had spoilt it all by using the nickname people called Selina when they were trying to annoy her.

'Was she trying to say she didn't take your diary?'

'No. She just said she thought it was nice of Nan to come and talk to us. That it would be a help.'

'What's wrong with her? She must have had a brainstorm!'

'I thought it was nice of her. I wish she could be like that all the time. In fact, I'm beginning to think it wasn't her who took the diary.'

'What makes you say that?' Laura said, sharply. 'I'd have thought it was obvious.'

Laura sounded so confident she made Hannah waver for a moment in her new friendly attitude to

Selina. Then she said, 'I don't think she'd have said that about Nan if she'd taken it. I think she'd have been too ashamed.'

'Well, I think it was her. She's always been spiteful.'

'Perhaps other people have made her like that. Calling her names and everything. She didn't know anyone when she came to this school and no one has tried to make friends with her.'

'So—you're gonna try, are you?'

'If she'll talk to me. Why not?'

'You're out of your tree. Well, don't blame me if she bites your head off. Don't say I didn't warn you! And you can count me out!'

Just after Hannah arrived home from school, Nan called in and Hannah was able to tell her what Selina had said.

'She was really grateful,' Hannah told her. 'She didn't know much about the school before 'cos she's new. She said she's got a much better idea about it now.'

Hannah's Dad came in the middle of her story and stood listening.

'Ah, yes. How did it go today? Did you have to give anyone the cane?'

'Funny you should say that,' said Nan. 'That was

the question that came up most often. Every class I went into the children said, "Did you have the cane?"'

'And did you?' Hannah's Dad laughed.

'No, I didn't, but I know someone who did!' Nan pulled a face at him.

'I didn't have the cane,' he protested. 'I don't think we had one. I had the ruler on my hand once or twice!'

'Ooh! What did you have that for?' Hannah asked.

'Can't remember now. Nothing like the things you get up to today.'

'I don't get up to anything!' Hannah said, then remembering the incident of the black bag, 'Nothing much anyway.'

'What sort of things did you tell them about?' asked her Dad.

'Oh, just what kind of lessons we had, how the school had altered. The children asked a lot of good questions. It's easier then—you just have to answer them. One of them asked if we had music and movement and they were astounded when I told them we didn't have a radio in the school.'

'I remember doing that,' said Dad. 'Standing in the middle of the hall trying to act like a tree in the wind. I felt really stupid.'

Nan laughed as he stood on one leg and waved his arms about. 'They didn't know the boys and girls were in separate schools either,' she said.

'Were they? We were all in together when I was there.'

'Just shows how much things change in a generation! There were no school dinners when I was there. Everyone went home to lunch—quite a long break if I remember rightly: about an hour and a half.'

'I hated school meals. The mashed potatoes were cooked early in the morning, then packed in those aluminium trays. Yuk! They tasted horrible.'

'Mmm. No wonder you were always starving by teatime; I don't think you ate much during the day.'

'I used to like being milk monitor. When there was any over we used to drink it.'

'We had to pay for our milk in my day. Tuppence-ha'penny for the week. Just imagine, a halfpenny for a third of a pint.'

'We didn't have to pay, did we?'

'No. But I remember my Grandmother telling me that when she first went to school, they had to pay sixpence a week for their lessons. That was quite a lot of money in those days.'

'Yes, I suppose it was.'

'Did you have games lessons when you were in

Gladstone?' Nan asked. 'I don't remember washing any kit for you until you went to High School.'

'Yes. I played football. I never got in the team though. Not good enough. The girls played rounders while we had football.'

'The girls play rugby and football now,' Hannah said.

'I think those are much too rough for girls to play. The children asked me about P.E., but I don't remember having organised games when I was there.'

'But, altogether, the afternoon went well, did it? You were a bit apprehensive about doing it.'

'Yes, I think so. They're talking about having an Assembly with the children dressing up in Edwardian clothes and each one telling something about those times. That's in addition to the Centenary project. And Hannah seems to have made friends with Selina too, so that's another bonus.'

'A successful day then!'

'Yes, I think you can say that.'

Hannah was afraid Selina would have reverted to her old hostile manner next day, but was pleased when she actually smiled at her and told her she had started on her project.

'You can have a look at Great-Gran's diary too, if you want.' Hannah was surprised to hear herself offering. 'The bits about the school anyway. The other parts probably wouldn't interest you.'

'Oh, thanks! When can I see it?'

'I'll check with Mum first, then perhaps you'd like to come round.'

'Or you can come to my house!'

Hannah's heart gave a lurch. If she took the diary there, would she be luckier the second time round? But she didn't want to appear too eager, so she said, 'Whatever you want to do. I'll have a word with Mum. See what she says.'

Hannah's mother looked worried when Hannah broached the subject of Selina coming to look at the diary.

'I'm sorry, love. But with all this work I've got on at the moment, I can't possibly have children running round the house. It would be too distracting. Ask her another time, will you? She can come to tea then.'

Hannah was secretly pleased with this answer. She would prefer another visit to Selina's house to see if the ghostly children appeared.

Selina said, 'No problem. Mum said to ask you to our house, being you're going to help me with my project. When can you come? This afternoon? After school?'

'I'll have to tell Mum. Perhaps I can catch her when she meets Tim.'

Hannah raced across the playground, hoping to see her mother before she left with Tim, Selina following close on her heels. But according to one of the other mothers Hannah's mother had gone to the shops.

'Sorry,' Hannah said. 'Tell you what! I'll ask her when I get back. She won't be long. Probably run out of something.'

'Will you come today? I'll give you a ring when I get home.'

Hannah saw her mother and Tim crossing the road at the bottom of the hill.

'Selina wants me to go to her house so's she can look at the diary. Can I go? She's going to phone when she gets home.'

'Yes, I think that'll be all right. What time? After tea or what?'

'Dunno. I'll ask her when she rings.'

It was agreed that Hannah would go to Selina's house after tea when her Dad was home to see her across the busy road.

Hannah put Great-Gran's diary safely in the deep pocket of her jacket and buttoned the flap.

When she came back home she hoped to have something new to write in her own project.

Chapter 10

Hannah hurried down the street towards Selina's house, her fingers clutching the diary in her pocket, hoping that with this contact the children might appear again. But she reached Selina's house without a sign of them.

As she rang the doorbell and listened to the music of 'March of the Men of Harlech', Hannah felt quite disappointed not to have seen them playing in the street, but then she cheered up, reminding herself that her mission today was to see the inside of Great-Gran's house. It was a start.

Selina opened the door and welcomed Hannah with a beaming smile. What a difference it makes to her when she smiles, Hannah thought.

'Come in. We've just finished tea. Dad was a bit late today.'

She led Hannah through to the ultra-modern living room and, on seeing it again, Hannah was sure Great-Gran would not feel at home enough in these surroundings to make an appearance.

'Hullo again,' Mrs Grantham greeted her. 'It's good of you to help Selina with her project. She's been quite worried about it. She's cheered up no end since your Nan went to the school to give her talk.'

Hannah smiled back at her. 'Good,' she said. 'Nan said it would be selfish to keep everything to myself.'

'Selina tells me your family used to live in this house.'

'Yes. My Great-Gran, the one who wrote the diary, lived here when she was first married. But she lived next door when she was a little girl.'

'Well, what d'you know! It's a small world.'

'Yes, I wouldn't have known anything about her if I hadn't found the diary.'

'You found it?'

'Yes.' Hannah went on to tell Mrs Grantham how she had come across the diary in the bottom of the workbox. 'This is it,' she said, pulling it out of her pocket and handing it to Selina's mother.

Mrs Grantham opened it and read the inscription. 'What beautiful handwriting,' she said. 'So different from the way people write today. My writing's awful. I suppose we're all in too much of a hurry nowadays to take so much care.'

She gave the diary back to Hannah.

'Just let me clear the table and you can work here,' Mrs Grantham said. 'Or would you prefer to go up to Selina's room?'

Hannah looked at Selina, her eyebrows raised in question.

'Yes, upstairs. Shall we?'

Hannah nodded. The bedrooms might not be furnished in quite such a different style from Great-Gran's day.

But one look at the white fitted units which lined two walls made her realise that Great-Gran would be no more at home here than downstairs.

Selina pulled up a stool and placed it at the side of hers in front of the desk and they sat down. Hannah took out the diary and handed it to Selina.

'There are a few bits about the school in there, but some of it's everyday stuff that happened to her. You can read it all if you want. Sorry, but there's a couple of pages missing or ripped towards the end. Must have been when her little sister or brother got hold of it.'

'Oh, pity.' Selina said. 'Thank goodness Nathan doesn't do things like that now. He just pinches my stuff and uses it—and doesn't bring it back. You should see his bedroom! If we lose anything now, we know where to look for it. Anyway, I'll just have a look at this. You can play with my things if you like while I do it.' Selina gestured towards the books, photos and ornaments on the shelves in the recess and the toy chest standing underneath.

'Thanks,' Hannah said, getting up to see them closer.

She glanced out of the window at the long stretch of grass with its swing and slide standing in the middle. There were very few plants growing in the borders, only a couple of straggly rose bushes which were trying to compete with the weeds.

Next door, however, was a profusion of colour with scarcely room to walk between the flowers that even trailed over the path.

'Who lives next door?' she asked.

'Which way?' Then as Hannah showed her, Selina said. 'Oh, that's Mrs Chamberlain. Pretty garden, isn't it? She's promised Dad some plants, but he never seems to get round to doing the garden. He's always too busy. And the way Nathan races around there on his bike, there's not even much grass left.'

'How long has she lived there?'

'Oh, ages. She's very old, and everything is so old-fashioned! She hasn't even got central heating. Still lights the coal fire in the winter. She must be freezing.'

Hannah felt her excitement grow at Selina's words. How could she get to know Mrs Chamberlain well enough to be invited into her house?

'Do you ever go in there?'

'I've been in a couple of times. Mum does some shopping for her occasionally. Mum says she's very independent, though.'

'Oh, I wish I could talk to her.'

'What for?'

'Well, if she's that old, perhaps she could tell us something about the school. She might have gone there,' Hannah added as she saw the sceptical look on Selina's face.

'Oh, yes. Never thought of that!'

'Can we knock the door and ask?' Now she'd had the idea, Hannah couldn't wait to find out.

'What would we say to her?'

'Just ask her, that's all!'

'I'd better ask my mother first. She might not like it.'

'Come on then.'

Hannah was out of the door and halfway down the stairs before Selina could object.

Mrs Grantham was filling the dishwasher when Hannah entered the kitchen and for a moment she hesitated, unsure how to broach the subject of meeting Mrs Chamberlain. Selina came up beside her.

'Mum, do you know if Mrs Chamberlain went to Gladstone when she was young?' she asked.

'Haven't a clue,' her mother replied. 'Why do you ask? Is it something to do with your project?'

'Hannah just had the idea, that's all. She could tell us what kind of clothes they wore in those days, stuff like that.'

'She might be able to, but I don't know if she went to your school, I'm afraid.'

'How old is she?' Hannah asked.

'Over eighty. I know she gets the extra pension.'

Not as old as Great-Gran would have been, thought Hannah. But she didn't really need extra information about the school; all she wanted was to get into her house to see if the past would come to life again.

'Go and see if she's in her garden,' Mrs Grantham said. 'She often puts in an hour or two out there in the evening after tea.'

Hannah and Selina rushed out into the garden and climbed up on to the top of the slide so they could see into next door's garden.

Mrs Chamberlain was bent over the side garden pulling up weeds. She looked up, caught sight of the girls and smiled.

'Hullo,' she said. 'What are you doing up there? Come to see my pretty flowers?'

'They're lovely,' Hannah said. 'But we're doing a project in school and we wondered if you could help us?'

'I'm sorry, m'dear. You'll have to speak up. I'm a bit hard of hearing.'

Hannah tried again, but still Mrs Chamberlain couldn't hear her question.

'Why not come round the front and I'll let you in.'

This was just what Hannah had hoped for and without more ado, the two girls descended the slide and went back indoors.

'Mum, Mrs Chamberlain asked us to go in. She couldn't hear what we were saying.'

'Oh, all right, but don't make a nuisance of yourselves. Remember, she's an old lady. She won't want to be bothered with a lot of questions.'

Chapter 11

The two girls ran to the front of the house and waited patiently for Mrs Chamberlain to open the door.

After a few moments and hearing no movement from within, Selina peered through the heavy black letter box.

'Isn't she coming?' asked Hannah.

'Not yet. She takes ages to come to the door.'

Hannah raised the old iron knocker and banged twice.

'Perhaps she's changed her mind,' Selina said, as she kicked impatiently at a paving stone.

'She did say "come round the front", didn't she?' Hannah asked.

'Yes, I'm sure she did.'

They waited, undecided what to do, then Hannah bent down and looked through the letter box.

The passageway was dark and a heavy curtain cut off the view to the other half of the hallway. Just as she was about to straighten up again, Mrs Chamberlain shuffled into view. Hannah let the flap drop and stood up.

'She's coming,' she said.

They waited expectantly, listening to the slow footsteps approaching the front door. At last it opened and Mrs Chamberlain stood there smiling at them.

'Now, what can I do for you? You'll have to speak up, I'm afraid. I'm a little hard of hearing.'

They explained what they wanted and Mrs Chamberlain stood aside.

'You'd better come in. We don't want to stand on the old step talking, do we? Let's go in and sit down.'

The two girls followed her through the dark passageway to the living room at the back of the house.

Looking about her, Hannah felt a thrill of excitement. This house couldn't have been altered since Great-Gran lived here.

The walls were papered halfway up with a thick, raised paper which had been varnished a deep brown, and the flowered print on the top half of the room was yellow with age. Heavy red chenille curtains hung at each side of the window which looked out on to a white-washed wall. And the fireplace! With its open fire, hobs to keep things warm and the oven at the side, it must be the same one Great-Gran had talked about in her diary—the one she'd had to clean out in her lunchtime!

'Sit down m'dears, and tell me what I can do for you.'

Hannah perched on the edge of a large wooden armchair, the cushion of which slid about as she sat down. Selina seated herself on a wooden stool at the side of the fireplace knocking against the long brass tongs and shovel and making them clang against the steel fender.

'Oh, sorry,' she said, apologetically, to Mrs Chamberlain.

'Don't worry about that. They won't break.'

'We just wanted to ask you if you went to Gladstone School.' Hannah began.

'The one at the top of the Terrace? No, my dear. I didn't come to Cardiff until, let me see it was 1954—or was it 1958? I'm not sure. I went to school in Aberdare, and we only moved here when my husband left his job in the pit. Better job down here, see. He got taken on in the steel works. Good pay and not so dangerous.'

'Oh!' Selina's disappointment could be heard in her voice.

'Why did you want to know that?'

'We're doing a project in school—you know, what the school was like years ago and we thought you might be able to tell us something.'

'Well, I can tell you we had to toe the line in them days. None of this mollycoddling you get nowadays. I had to walk miles to get to school. No school bus or cars then, I can tell you. And the teachers were very strict. You had to mind your Ps and Qs. Oh yes. The cane came out if you misbehaved.'

Hannah's eyes had been roving round the room as she listened to Mrs Chamberlain's conversation with Selina, taking in the heavy iron kettle that sang on the hob, the line stretched below the mantelpiece airing a pair of Mrs Chamberlain's thick lisle stockings. A fringed cloth edged with bobbles draped the mantelshelf, while a black slate clock ticked a loud accompaniment to their voices.

'Was the house just like this when you moved here?' Hannah asked.

'What? Oh, yes. I don't need all this central heating they have now. Gets too stuffy. No wonder people catch so many colds. Too much of a change when they go outside. Me, now, I never catch cold. Good food inside you, that's the thing. Give me a nice drop of *cawl* and a crust of bread on a cold day and you can keep all your hot burgers or whatever you call 'em.'

Hannah smiled at the old lady's words.

'The reason I asked is that my Great-Grandmother used to live in this house and I wondered if this it how it looked when she lived here.'

'Well, well, now. I didn't know that! It's a small world, isn't it? How long ago was that?'

'I know it was during the First World War, because I found the diary she wrote when she was ten and she writes things about the war and that.

114

But I think she probably lived here for a long time after that.'

'I know an old lady lived here before I did. She died, I believe, and they left some of her things here. Those fire dogs, for instance: they were hers.'

'Did she leave anything else behind? Anything personal, I mean.'

'Funny you should say that. Not so long ago I was looking for something in the dresser drawer. My sharp knife had dropped down the back and I had to pull the drawer out. I found this.' Mrs Chamberlain pushed herself out of her chair and, reaching behind the clock, took out a bunch of envelopes and papers. Sorting through them, she selected one.

'What was your Great-Gran's name? Her first name.'

'Rose. It's written in the front of the diary, see?' Hannah took the diary out of her pocket.

Mrs Chamberlain handed the envelope to Hannah. 'This'll be hers then. You might as well have it.'

Hannah lifted the flap on the yellowed envelope and looked inside. It was a card of some description. She slid it out, and saw a postcard embroidered in coloured silks, with the message, 'A Kiss from France'.

'Oh, isn't it pretty? Look, Selina, it's the French flag and the Union Jack. And look at the flowers!'

She turned it over and saw written on the back 'To Rosie Pink from Frank.'

'He did write to her then,' Hannah said, her eyes glowing. 'Oh, I am glad. She would have been miserable if he hadn't.'

'I'm glad your visit wasn't such a disappointment after all,' Mrs Chamberlain said.

'Disappointment! Oh, no,' Hannah said. 'It's been wonderful to see the house just as it was when Great-Gran lived in it. Thank you very much for letting us see it—and especially for this,' Hannah tapped the envelope. 'I'll put it with her diary.' Impulsively, she bent forward and kissed Mrs Chamberlain's wrinkled cheek. 'Thanks.'

Mrs Chamberlain beamed with pleasure. 'Come again. Any time you like. I'm usually in.'

Hannah was pleased to know that she had an open invitation to visit the old lady whenever she wanted to. It would be almost like visiting Great-Gran.

As the two girls walked ahead of Mrs Chamberlain towards the front door, Hannah glanced through the open front-room door, noticing the large picture of a sailing ship battling through towering waves which hung over the mantelpiece and the vase of tall grasses standing between yet another set of brass fire irons in the grate.

Then she saw the young girl sitting in one of the rexine-covered armchairs at the side of the fireplace, a handkerchief held to her eyes. It was Great-Gran! But she looked so sad, and an older woman was stroking the hair back from her forehead as if trying to comfort her.

Hannah recognised the lady. It was Great-Gran's mother. Nan had shown her some photographs recently and there was no mistaking the strong nose and deep-set eyes, or the hair parted in the middle and looped back to the nape of her neck in a bun.

What was wrong? As she watched, Rose opened her hand and looked at something she held. It was the card Mrs Chamberlain had just given her.

With a shock, Hannah remembered the war. It was obvious that something had happened to the soldier who had sent the card. As she watched, the girl stood up, a look of determination on her face. She hugged her mother for a moment, then squaring her shoulders, walked right past Hannah and up the stairs.

When Hannah looked back into the room, it was empty. Selina gave her a little push.

'Go on, then. What're you waiting for?'

'Sorry, er, I was just looking at that picture.'

'It's nice, isn't it?' Mrs Chamberlain had caught them up. 'That was another thing your family left here. I don't know if it's valuable. I know it's too big for this room, but people went in for that sort of thing years ago—and I like it.'

'Yes,' Hannah agreed, still dazed from her latest encounter with the past.

'And don't forget now. Come and see me again. Any time. I don't get many visitors.'

'Did you really like that picture?' Selina asked. 'It was very dark. You could hardly see what it was supposed to be.'

'Yes. It was O.K.' Hannah wondered vaguely if she had seen the picture in its original colours, because it had been quite clear when she looked at it. Of course, she had been seeing it through the eyes of the past: that must be it.

'We didn't get much out of her, did we?' Selina sighed.

'What! Oh, nothing about the school, but I got a lot. Fancy that card being at the back of the drawer. It's a wonder it wasn't found ages ago. Lucky for me it wasn't. Anyone else might have thrown it out.'

'What's so good about an old card?'

'Don't you see? You read the diary! It's the one Frank sent her—the boy who went to fight in France. Remember? He promised.'

'Oh, I see, I didn't take much notice of that. I was looking for things about the school.'

Hannah hugged the diary with the precious card close to her. Perhaps Great-Gran had hidden the card, too. Perhaps she had even guided her to it.

Chapter 12

After saying goodbye to Selina and her mother, Hannah hurried to Nan's house. She couldn't wait to show her the card and tell her what she'd seen.

Nan was in her front garden, watering the tubs of flowers.

'Hello! Where have you been?'

'You'll never guess! You know I told you how much nicer Selina was after you'd been to tell everyone about the school?'

Nan nodded.

'Well—she asked me to go to her house this afternoon!'

'And . . ?'

'Look what Mrs Chamberlain gave me. She's the old lady who lives in the house next door now.' Hannah took the card out of the diary and handed it to Nan.

'What is it?' Nan turned it over and read the inscription on the back.

'To Rosie Pink from Frank.' A frown creased Nan's forehead. 'Is this . . . ?'

'Yes! Mrs Chamberlain found it at the back of her dresser drawer the other day. It must have been there ever since Great-Gran left.'

'How strange.'

'And that's not all. When we were coming out of her house, I just happened to glance into the front room—and you'll never guess!'

'What? Come on, don't keep me in suspense!'

'I saw her again—and her mother!'

Nan looked impressed. 'It's funny how she always appears to you.'

'It's true. I'm not making it up. She was sitting in the armchair—she was crying, and her mother was making a fuss of her. You know, smoothing her hair away from her forehead. Then she got up and walked right past me. It was weird!'

'I wonder what was wrong?'

'Well, she was holding this card in her hand and crying. So I think it was probably something to do with that soldier.'

'Mmm, possibly. War's a terrible thing. I remember when I was about your age, they'd been saying that we might have to go to war with Germany and I, being young and silly, imagined soldiers in armour riding on white horses into battle, even though I'd heard all about the terrible things that happened in the First World War.'

'What was it like really?'

'Oh, having to queue for food, running to the shelter at night and listening for bombs dropping— or hopefully the All Clear siren.'

'Were you scared, Nan?'

'I can't remember being afraid—at least, only once when the landmine dropped in Cathays Terrace. I expected to see our house a pile of rubble when we got out. But all we found was that a ceiling in the middle bedroom had come down.'

'You never heard what happened to Frank, then?'

'No. My mother only ever told me about this card—she said he used to call her Rosie Pink. I wonder if that was what put the idea into her head about being a nurse?'

'Oh, was she a nurse? I didn't know.'

'No, I'm afraid she had to give up that idea. In those days you had to pay for your training and it cost more than my grandparents could afford. But she made up for it later, when we were all grown up. She joined the Red Cross and really enjoyed it. I've got all her certificates upstairs somewhere. I'll dig them out one day and show them to you.'

'That wouldn't be the same as working in a hospital though, would it? She must have been disappointed.'

'She did work in a hospital. She did voluntary work and loved it. She helped in the baby clinic and the chiropody clinic and even had a couple of sessions on the wards. She was thrilled to bits!'

'I wish I was writing about Great-Gran instead of the school, really. I know lots more about her.'

'You could do both. Write down everything you find out about her—a sort of record for the family and I'll put it with the family tree when I've finished it.'

'I haven't done the school project yet. I suppose I'd better find out what the opening date was and things like that.'

'Have you been to the Library? There's a place in the Central Library that might be able to help you.'

'No, not yet. But everybody else will have all that stuff and I wanted something different.'

'Well, it's the sort of thing you must put in. Then the more personal things will spice it up a bit. What about your other friend? Laura? How is she getting on?'

'She's not speaking to me. She didn't like it 'cos I went to Selina's house.'

'You girls! I don't know why you can't all be friends together.'

'I'd like to be, but—I don't know. I suppose it's because the other kids don't like Selina and Laura's afraid they won't like her if she's friends with Selina.' Hannah sighed.

'Never mind, it'll all come out in the wash.'

Hannah laughed: Nan had some funny sayings.

As she walked home, she wondered how she could get back on good terms with Laura and still stay friends with Selina. She knew Selina hadn't been the one who'd thrown her diary in the black bag: she had been too thrilled when Hannah had let her read it. And if she'd been the one who had taken it, she could have kept it and read it for as long as she wanted. Who could it have been? If she could solve that and prove to Laura that Selina hadn't done it, perhaps they could all be friends! She'd have to find a way. Someone must know who did it.

She told Selina what she thought as they walked across the playground next day.

'You mean, you thought I'd taken it? Why would I do that?'

'Well . . .' Hannah was embarrassed now. It was one thing to think something, but quite another to explain why she had thought it.

'Well,' she tried again, 'you hadn't been very friendly and you sort of seemed the obvious person. I don't think it was you now, though.'

Selina was silent for a few moments and Hannah thought to herself, now I've upset Selina as well. I won't have any friends left soon.

'I'm sorry,' she said, stopping to face Selina. 'I shouldn't have jumped to conclusions. Are we still friends?'

''Course. But I'd better tell you what I know

now. See, I saw her take it. I thought it was a joke. But when Miss Edwards said it was missing, I didn't know what to do. The kids don't like me much, I know. They make fun of my hair—but I can't help the colour: I hate it. I've even thought of dyeing it black or something.'

'Who took it? Who was she?'

'I didn't want to say. They'd be calling me names for telling tales, then.'

'Who? Tell me who?'

Selina gulped nervously. 'Laura!'

'What? You sure?'

'Yes. She took it out of your pocket—your jacket was on the back of the chair. It was when you went over to help clear up that paint they spilled. She looked around to see if anyone was looking, but they were all around William's table, so she ran over and put it in the black bag. She did: I saw her!'

'I wish you'd told me before.'

'I wanted to, but I was too scared. And I couldn't believe it when I saw her "helping" you to look for it and clear up afterwards.'

'Mmm, she did, didn't she? Why?'

'Perhaps she was sorry she'd done it and wanted to make up for it.'

'Possibly.' Hannah thought for a minute. 'What am I going to do now?'

'You gonna tell her what I said?'

'I don't know. I don't know what to do. I didn't think she'd do a thing like that.'

'I expect she was jealous because you had that diary and she thought you'd win the prize. I know I was.'

'Yes, but you didn't steal it, did you? If it wasn't for Great-Gran I wouldn't have got it back. I'd never have thought of looking in that black bag for it.'

'What d'you mean? How did your Great-Gran get it back for you?'

Hannah hesitated. She'd already told Laura about the things she'd seen and look how she'd repaid her. But Selina was different: she really seemed to like reading about the things that happened in the past.

She made up her mind and told Selina how Great-Gran had appeared to her in her bedroom and had pointed to a black bag with a streak of paint down the side.

'Honest? You're not joking?'

'Cross my heart.'

'Weren't you scared?'

'No.' She almost added, 'I've never been afraid when Great-Gran appears', but stopped herself in time.

'Perhaps you dreamed it.'

Remembering that Nan had told her that some people might not understand, Hannah thought it best not to tell Selina that she had seen into the past more than once, so she replied, 'Perhaps, but she led me to it, didn't she?'

Chapter 13

When she went to bed that night, Hannah thought and thought about how she could tackle Laura about taking the diary. Thinking back over the events that led to its discovery in the black bag, her eyes strayed to the corner of her bedroom where Great-Gran had appeared. If only she would come back and help her again.

Suddenly, an idea came into her head. She could pretend to Laura that Great-Gran had told her the name of the culprit. Yes, that should do it.

She fell asleep planning exactly what she would say to make Laura own up.

Next day, as she walked across the playground and saw Laura standing in the corner of the yard all alone, her nerve almost failed her. But she spurred herself on. She must do it; she had to know.

'Hi!' she said, walking up to her former friend as casually as she could.

'Hi!' Laura said, in a wary tone. 'Where's Selina this morning?'

'She's not here yet. Anyway, it's you I wanted to see.'

'Oh, I thought you'd soon get tired of her.'

Exasperated, Hannah said, 'Why do you have to

be like that? Why can't we all be friends? She's very nice when you get to know her. Give her a chance!'

'No thanks. Is that what you wanted to see me about?'

'No.' Hannah recognised defeat. She'd never convince Laura. 'I wanted to tell you something. It's about the time my diary went missing.' As she spoke, Hannah watched Laura carefully. She became very still, a watchful, wary look in her eyes.

'Ye-es. What about it?'

'I know who put it in the bin bag.'

A frightened expression flashed into Laura's eyes for a moment, then defiance set her lips in a straight line and she tilted her chin and glared at Hannah.

'Yeah?'

'You know I told you Great-Gran told me where it was? Well, you can guess the rest. She must have known I was worried about it. Wondering who could hate me enough to throw it away like that.'

Laura's face flushed and she looked about to cry. Hannah almost felt sorry for her.

'It wasn't fair,' she muttered. 'You knew everything about the school from that—and you were sucking up to Miss Edwards. I didn't mean to do it; it was just there. I was sorry afterwards, honest. Well, I helped you find it, didn't I? And I helped you clear up the mess.'

'There wouldn't have been a mess if you hadn't taken it in the first place. You could have read it if you'd asked, but you weren't interested, were you? You said a new doll was better than an old diary. So why throw it away if it was so useless? I would never have found it again if it hadn't been for Great-Gran.'

'What did she say?' Laura's curiosity overcame her feeling of guilt.

'She didn't have to say anything; she just let me know.'

Laura looked puzzled for a moment, then said, 'What you gonna do now? Tell Miss, I s'pose!'

'What would you do if you were me?'

Laura shuffled her feet and gave Hannah an agonised look. 'I dunno—but I said I'm sorry. What more can I do?'

Then Hannah had what she thought was a brilliant idea. 'You can make friends with Selina, and try to get everybody else to be friends too.'

Laura hesitated, then said, 'O.K. I'll try—but I can't promise anything for the rest of 'em.'

Selina caught up with Hannah as they went into the cloakroom. 'I saw you talking to Laura,' she said. 'What did she say?'

Hannah grinned. 'You were right. She owned up.'

'How did you get her to do that?'

'I made her think Great-Gran had told me who

had done it and she probably thought she'd come back and haunt her if she didn't own up.'

Selina laughed. 'Let's hope she doesn't try anything like that again.'

'I don't think she will.' She spoke in such a serious tone that Selina looked at her questioningly. 'She's afraid I'll tell Miss Edwards.'

Later that day, Miss Edwards asked Hannah if she had any photographs of Great-Gran or her family. 'We'd like to put them up on a board so that all the school can see them,' she explained. 'Also, we're going to have a special assembly when the topic will be about the early days of the school, so any information you or your Nan can supply will be useful.'

Hannah called in to see Nan on her way home from school and asked her about the photographs.

'Have you got anything?' she asked.

'Loads,' said Nan. 'There're all in a big biscuit tin. I'll sort them out for you, shall I?'

'Can I help?'

'Yes. Come over after tea and we'll sort them out together.'

There must have been hundreds of photographs in the biscuit tin, but the ones Hannah was most interested in were in the album.

There was one of an old lady dressed in a long black silk dress, a tiny black bonnet perched on top of the sparse grey hair that was scraped away from her face and gave it a stern look. Her hands were clasped over a drawstring purse in her lap.

'That's Great-Gran's grandmother,' Nan said. 'She looks formidable, doesn't she?'

When Hannah turned the page and saw the picture of the young girl in a white dress and a picture hat, holding a spray of flowers, she gave a startled cry.

'What's the matter?' asked Nan.

'It's Great-Gran! Just like she described herself in the diary.'

'Yes, and these are her brothers and sisters. I put them all on the same page, to try and get some order into them. These are the oldest ones I've got in this album. I'm fitting faces to names on the family tree.'

Hannah studied the old photographs. There was one of a group of boys outside the boiler house railings in the playground. They all wore stiff white collars with rounded edges, dark jackets and trousers that seemed to be tucked into black socks just below the knee.

Another of a girl in a plaid dress with long ringlets over her shoulders looked very like the girl she had seen on the swing in the street.

She gave a deep sigh, 'I don't suppose you'd let me take these to school, would you?'

'As long as they're looked after. Although perhaps it would be better if I had them photocopied. Yes, that would be best. Now, let's see which ones would be best.'

They sorted out half a dozen pictures and some old Attendance Cards that were mixed in with them and Nan promised to have them done the next day.

'Have you finished your project yet?' asked Nan.

'Not yet. I've been writing all I've found out about Great-Gran to go with your family tree.'

'When does it have to be in?'

'By the twentieth.'

'That's next week.'

'It's not, is it? And I haven't found out anything about when the school was opened yet—or coloured in the cover.'

'You'd better get down to it, then. Time's running out.'

'I will,' promised Hannah. 'I'll start as soon as I get home.'

Chapter 14

Hannah worked for two hours that night and only reluctantly put away her project when her mother insisted that it was time to go to bed.

'But I'll never get it finished in time,' she moaned.

'Get up a bit earlier. You'll be fresher then.'

When Hannah woke next morning, her throat was sore and she felt very hot and ached all over.

'No school for you today. I'll take a note to your teacher to tell her you're not well,' her mother said.

'But I can't stay home, I've got too much to do. And I said I'd pick up those photocopies from Nan's on the way home.'

'I'll do that for you. But in the meantime, stay in bed. If you're no better in an hour or two, I'll send for the doctor.'

Hannah tried to write some more of her project, but her head ached and her eyes watered and she had to give up in the end. Tears of frustration rolled down her cheeks. Oh, why hadn't she got on with it instead of trying to find out more about Great-Gran? It would be finished by now if she had only put her mind to it. She imagined all the others with well-researched, perfectly presented projects and hers would be awful, even though she'd had Great-

Gran's diary to help her. She turned on her side and pulled the duvet up over her head.

Later that day her mother brought in the photocopied pictures saying, 'Nan had two sets taken in case you'd like to use one in your project.'

Hannah cheered up when she saw how well they had come out.

'I'll take them to school tomorrow,' she said.

'We'll see,' her mother said. 'It all depends how well you are. It's Friday, so perhaps it would be better if you stayed in over the weekend.'

'But, Mum,' Hannah protested.

'You can hand your project in on Monday. I asked Miss Edwards about it and she said it was due in then.'

'But I haven't been to the library or anything.'

'You shouldn't have left everything to the last moment. You're always the same. And even if you were well enough, I haven't got time to take you into town this weekend; I've got too much on—and so has Dad.'

Hannah spent Saturday and Sunday working on the cover of her folder. She coloured in the graphics, then cut them out and stuck them in a border around the edge. Then she painstakingly made a half circle out of the letters in the school's name with the date of opening and the centenary date underneath, then painted them in the dark red colours of the school.

In a last attempt for more information, she rang Nan and, after thanking her for the photocopies, asked her if she was sure there was nothing else she could remember.

'I think I've told you everything,' she said, and there was silence for a moment at the other end of the phone. 'Did I tell you about the time during the war when we were running across the playground to the air raid shelter and we could see bombs actually falling from a plane over the docks? Oh, that wouldn't be any good: that was when I was in the High School.'

'Weren't you scared? Was anyone killed? What did you do?'

'We dived into the shelter. We had to; the teachers made sure of that—and when anything like that happens, you don't have time to feel scared: you just get on with it. But I heard later that some dockers working on a ship were killed. I was very upset. It seemed to bring the war very close.

'But that was a long time ago. More to the point, how are you now? Better?'

'Much better, thank you. And if you think of anything else before Monday, will you let me know?'

'Of course I will. But it was so long ago that only certain things stand out in my mind.'

After she had put the phone down, Hannah remembered the photographs Nan had copied. Yes, it would be a good idea to cut them out and stick them in her project to show how people dressed in those days.

On Monday, when Hannah handed in her folder with the rest of the class, she was relieved to see that most people's projects were not as bulky as hers and she was quite convinced that her cover stood out from the rest.

She handed the other copies of the photographs over to Miss Edwards, who took them thankfully saying, 'I'll put them up on the notice board in the Hall where the rest of the memorabilia is going. Have you seen the picture of the school taken when there were no traffic lights out there? And no traffic for that matter! Just a solitary horse and cart plodding its way up the road.'

Later on, Hannah and some of the others in her class were given parts to learn for the special Assembly which was to take place at the end of the following week.

Several of the mothers who were clever with their needles had agreed to make frilled pinafores for the girls to wear over their dresses and people were asked to bring anything they might have dating back to the early nineteen hundreds.

Nan had two old cast-iron flat irons which she

lent to Hannah with the warning, 'They're heavy—mind you don't drop them on your toes!'

The night before the Assembly, Hannah's hair was put in curling rags, just the way Great-Gran had described Margaret's being done, so that her hair would fall in ringlets on her shoulders.

Her class was performing a sketch based on the time they visited St Fagans. Tom had six strokes of the cane for putting his hand up when he didn't know the answer to a question and Hannah had to wear the 'Welsh Not' around her neck for breaking into Welsh when answering hers.

Everybody laughed when Huw, the tallest boy in the class, gave a good impersonation of their teacher as he stormed up and down in front of them, banging a ruler on the desk as he shouted.

Another group used the household tools to show how mats had to be hung on the washing line, then beaten with a kind of wicker bat and brushed after wet tea leaves had been scattered on them. Clothes were thumped up and down in a dolly tub, put through a huge mangle to squeeze the water out and then pressed with the irons Hannah had brought—after they had been 'heated' in front of a fire made out of red crepe paper.

At the end of Assembly, Mr Harris thanked everyone who had taken part or brought items for them to use, then said, 'Will those who took part in the sketches remain behind, please. We have a photographer waiting who is going to take you in your groups, so just sit down quietly while all the rest file out.'

They were posed in a tableau for each sketch. Hannah almost expected to see a photographer with an old fashioned camera, the kind she'd seen in old films, the type which had to be lit before the flash exploded into light.

'Fold your costumes up tidily,' Mrs Edwards said. 'Don't forget we're going to do it all again for the parents next week.'

'I hadn't heard that before,' Hannah said.

'You were away. They told us last Friday,' Selina said. 'They're going to announce the winner of the prize at the same time.'

'I couldn't finish mine properly,' said Hannah miserably. 'I should have gone to the library last Saturday, but I had to stay in because I wasn't well.'

'You're sure to win. Everybody says so. You've got all that stuff about your Great-Granny.'

'You saw that as well. I showed it to you. Other people have probably got more than me now.' She hoped it wasn't true, but it sounded likely.

'Laura's been telling everyone that she knows someone who came to the school and has told her loads and loads of stuff.'

'Mmm, I bet. She's like that. Always got to know more than other people.' But Hannah felt a little shiver of anxiety. If she didn't win the prize she'd feel she'd let Great-Gran down, but it was too late now to do anything about it. She'd just have to wait and see.

The day of the special Assembly came at last. Hannah, looking through the Hall doors, could see her Mum sitting next to Selina's mother, deep in conversation.

Mr Harris was in a very happy mood, as if the children's excitement were catching. Introducing the sketches, he told the parents how hard all the children had worked on the Assembly and their projects.

'We'll be announcing the winner at the end of this Assembly,' he said. 'Also, the photographs of our school performance of these sketches have come back and if anyone would like to order them, please add your names to the list on the notice board next to them.'

Hannah glanced across and saw the coloured prints; she'd take a look at them afterwards.

As they played their parts, Hannah had a strange unreal feeling that they were not taking part in a sketch, but actually living in those times. I've been thinking too much about Great-Gran, she thought, when she imagined she saw her out of the corner of her eye, sitting at a desk in the classroom scene and almost forgot to come in on cue to answer her question.

At last the final sketch was performed and Mr Harris was up on his feet, acknowledging the applause. When all was quiet again, he said, 'I would now like to announce the winner of our prizes for the Centenary/Millennium project.'

Hannah's stomach lurched.

'The prize for the Lower school goes to Amanda Bright. Well done, Amanda. A very good project with plenty of drawings and colouring in it. Well done!'

Mr Harris waited while a small girl from year three came up to receive her prize.

'The prize for the Upper school goes to a girl who is quite new to the school. She only came here last term, but she appears to have learned more about the school than anyone else. He held up a folder which was bulging with paper. 'So if Selina Grantham will come forward, I'll present her with her prize.'

Selina have a gasp of surprise and turned to look at Hannah.

'Go on then,' Hannah said, smiling at her and giving her a little push. 'Go and get it.'

Selina walked up on to the stage and Mr Harris presented the box with the CD player in it to her.

She came back down smiling, but with a dazed look on her face.

Hannah bit back her disappointment. She'd half expected not to win, but now it had actually happened, she felt near to tears.

'Congratulations. How did you get so much?' Hannah whispered.

'Went to the Archives last week.'

Hannah frowned. She'd never heard of such a place.

Mr Harris was speaking again. 'There is one young lady who has helped many of the others in her class by sharing information she had in her possession. I would like to thank Hannah and ask her to come forward to receive a small gift to show our appreciation.'

It was Selina's turn to nudge Hannah and she stumbled up on to the stage with her mind in a whirl. Mr Harris was presenting her with a cassette player. They must have known she'd broken hers! This was something she hadn't expected at all. The disappointment of not winning the CD player was completely gone, and she beamed at the audience as they gave her a good clap.

'Years ago, in your Great-Gran's time, your prize would probably have been a book, but we've brought things up-to-date! You can even listen to books being read on this.'

Hannah thanked Mr Harris through her smiles and went back to her seat.

'I'd also like to place on record our thanks to Hannah's Gran. You will all have met her when she came to tell you what the school was like when she was here.'

There was more applause and this time Hannah joined in.

Afterwards, they all gathered round the board where their photographs were displayed. People who had not been at all friendly with Selina before were making a fuss of her and asking to see her prize. Even Laura was joining in. Hannah felt a rush of pleasure that; at last, Selina was making new friends.

She studied the photographs on the board. Who was that girl sitting at the desk next to her? She'd been sitting alone, she was sure! She looked closer. Although the image was a bit fuzzy, as if the person had moved when the picture was taken, she could see a strong resemblance to the pictures of Great-Gran as a girl. Hannah chuckled to herself. It seemed that Great-Gran had wanted to be in on the celebrations, too—and why not? If it hadn't been for her diary their Assembly might never have happened.